T5-AFF-583

At War with Mexico

Literature of the American West
WILLIAM KITTREDGE, General Editor

Other Books by Bruce Cutler

A West Wind Rises (Lincoln, 1962; Topeka, 1999)

Seeing the Darkness: Naples, 1943–1945 (Kansas City, 1998)

Afterlife (La Crosse, 1997)

The Massacre at Sand Creek: Narrative Voices (Norman, 1995)

(with Judson Jerome) *Two Long Poems* (La Crosse, 1991)

Dark Fire (Kansas City, 1985)

Nectar in a Sieve (La Crosse, 1985)

The Maker's Name (La Crosse, 1980)

The Doctrine of Selective Depravity (La Crosse, 1980)

A Voyage to America (Lincoln, 1967)

Sun City (Lincoln, 1964)

The Year of the Green Wave (Lincoln, 1960)

At War with Mexico

A FICTIONAL MOSAIC

Bruce Cutler

University of Oklahoma Press : Norman

Some of the characters depicted in this work bear a strong resemblance to their historical namesakes. While a number of their actions and statements are carefully reported, other actions, statements, and motivations are a matter of my conjecture. I have taken liberties in this area, as have many of the historians and commentators on this period whose work has stimulated me over the past four decades.

Published with the assistance of the National Endowment for the Humanities, a federal agency which supports the study of such fields as history, philosophy, literature, and language.

Library of Congress Cataloging-in-Publication Data

Cutler, Bruce, 1930–
    At war with Mexico : a fictional mosaic / Bruce Cutler.
      p. cm. — (Literature of the American West ; v. 6)
    ISBN 0-8061-3264-7 (alk. paper)
    1. Mexican War, 1846–1848—Fiction.   2. West (U.S.)—Fiction.
  3. Mexico—Fiction.   I. Title.   II. Series.

PS3553.U8 A92 2001
813'.54—dc21

                      00-044714

At War with Mexico: A Fictional Mosaic is Volume 6 in the Literature of the American West series.

The paper in this book meets the guidelines for permanence and durability of the Committee on Production Guidelines for Book Longevity of the Council on Library Resources, Inc. ∞

·1 2 3 4 5 6 7 8 9 10

This book is for Emily
in love and wonder

Contents

Preface

Americans have long since left behind their role as outsiders in history. I trace that transformation to the years of the war we waged against Mexico, years that were filled with a mixture of hope, ambition, piety, incomprehension, arrogance, and greed. It was a time in our government's history which Ralph Waldo Emerson characterized as that of a democracy turning into "a government of bullies tempered by [newspaper] editors"—with, of course, a small, articulate minority in opposition to its policies at every step of the way. Willy-nilly, it was at that time we acquired our national *persona,* one which continues to drive us, and dog us, both.

It was also a time when attitudes about the hierarchy of the races jelled with the enthusiastic participation of most of the respected scientists of the day. These were years in which God himself seemed to dictate the course of national events. We were becoming a nation whose white, Anglo-Saxon populace would be the "chosen people" of a new world age. By the same token, the future role of African American and Native American peoples was coming to look increasingly subservient, bleak, and hopeless.

This outlook and its consequences played out violently during the Civil War, and afterward, in the subversion of the fourteenth and fifteenth amendments to the Constitution and the wars conducted against the Plains Indians. They were a harbinger of attitudes that made possible one of the bloodiest conflicts in U.S. history, which came some fifty years later—our war to stifle the Philippine independence movement (1899–1902), in which somewhere between a quarter of a million and a million Filipinos died in the ruthless imposition of American rule.

♦ ♦

In writing this book I have been indebted to many who have written about these years in our nation's life. I have made liberal use of documents, literature, anecdotes, and oratory of the period. I have retold some of the well-known tales of the time, garbled some perfectly fine statements by the famous, clarified some of the obscure ones made by others, and perhaps fudged a date or two. Contrary to what may seem to be the case, I have actually taken few liberties in characterizing the scientific doctrines of the day as they were articulated by their most serious and distinguished exponents.

All this is by way of saying, there is history here, but there is much that is not. This book is a work of fiction, made up of fictional articles, dialogues, letters, and poems worked into a mosaic meant to be suggestive of the myths of the time.

Alfred de Musset, the French poet and playwright, once wrote: "How glorious it is—and also how painful—to be an exception." What else is our nation—and what has it ever been—but "an exception"?

I offer this book with a strong sense of the irony implicit in that question.

BRUCE CUTLER

Santa Cruz, California

At War with Mexico

1846

♦ ♦

To commit violent and unjust acts, it is not enough for a government to have the will or even the power. The habits, ideas, and passions of the times must lend themselves to their committal.

—ALEXIS DE TOCQUEVILLE

♦ ♦

There is no quicker way of getting the crowd to shout Hosannah than by riding into the city on the back of an ass.

—FRIEDRICH NIETZSCHE

♦ ♦

Giving It a Name

"Our Federal Union—one and indivisible."
So vowed Old Hickory. So are we bound.

Granting that, there are many Americas. The Old Colony,
with its Puritan solemnity of purpose. The South, with its
        flamboyant
past and burgeoning present. And now the Western
Commonwealth—our newest shining star!

                                        Call it
a cloud by day, or a pillar of fire by night,
an aura emanates from that vast Domain, dazzling
the eyes of rich and poor, merchant and farmer,
north and south alike. To each and all
it has unsealed a Covenant. It has found a voice
and speaks a tongue that all can understand.

                                And there is music.
Not just the songs arising from its myriad flocks—we hear
it humming with the spirit of Enterprise!

                        The soul of this country
has longed for decades for something more than talk—
talk of tariffs, talk of a national bank,
talk of internal improvements. Our soul has sought
a bright celestial beacon, one to stay
the nation's course. One to guide us to a future
worthy of ancient myth.

Now we have found it.
Its name? We might as well define infinity
or space. It shines with a diamond brilliance. And who
is so heartless not to have felt its power and the promise
of its glory?

We hereby name it: *Manifest Destiny!*

United States Magazine and Democratic Review
January 1846

An Announcement of a Sale

Price, Birch & Co. announce a very special
winter sale. Only the finest quality
stock. Every item guaranteed to be
in prime condition, coming from distant shores

and put up for sale for the first time ever here
in Washington City. The public viewing will be held
on Friday, to commence at ten A.M. Direct
from the public keep they will come by cart to the place
of auction where every physical detail may freely
be inspected. Bucks for fieldwork, wenches
for the house and breeding. A compliment of children, very
special! All to be seen and had this week!

Commercial Gazette
Washington, D.C.
January 1846

Westward Ho for California!

Andrew Jackson Grayson, a merchant of this state,
announces he will form an emigrant train
for California. A number of his friends have begged to go,
and he has given in to their entreaties.
He has consented to take command and thereby
pledges his life to those disposed to join him.
His wife and children will accompany. It is hoped therefore
the group will prove well-organized, industrious, and orderly.

Grayson is a man of determination, a man of enterprise,
one not accustomed to the affectations of city life
who has courted from his youth the dangers of the wilds
and deserts of the great Southwest. "Emigrants should provide
themselves with arms and ammunition, good teams of oxen,
and supplies of food for at least six months. No heavy
furniture, but farming implements and seeds." Three hundred
emigrants in seventy wagons will join the column,
including Colonel Russell, James Frazier Reed
of the Black Hawk War, Mister Francis Parkman
of Harvard College, and George and Jacob Donner
with their families. Says Grayson, "Who wants to go to California
without it costing them a cent? Eight young men who can drive
an ox will be accommodated by gentlemen in train.
Come on, boys! The government of California gives
away large tracts to immigrants. All the land
you want! And it doesn't cost a penny! So it's *Westward
Ho for the mountains, and on to California!*"

Saint Louis *Reveille*
February 1846

A Note from an
Adviser to the President

How recently have you sojourned in the city of New York?
Have you seen how the populace lives? I would not call
it living. By day they scuttle about the streets, down
to the piers, back and forth to the manufactures. Their faces
betray the weary half-soul that you see in dogs.

You must vow that for our youth there will come a change.
We are going to put a large investment in their future.
"Yes," the Whigs will say, "by taking half
of Mexico by war!" As if that government—frowzing
away its days, bankrupt and inept—had the slightest
power to turn one seashell on the coast of California
to its purpose!

                    Sir, it cannot be right that our young people
in the prime and very flower of their youth should spend
their days in cadging food and selling themselves
into servitude. Let us give them a place to go
to find a life, to learn self-discipline, to feel proud
of themselves. To stand tall on homesteads—on their own land!

It is you who must complete the work of Andrew
Jackson. You have a deep belief in the destiny
of this land. We are not to be a nation of a few
born rich and the many who are only deserving cases.
We are a fierce proud nation. We have whipped the British
and every European power that set its foot
upon our shores. Our frontiers will never be described

by insignificant rivers or marks at some obscure latitude.
Our borders will stretch from sea to sea. We
are a nation among nations. A nation to be reckoned with!

February 1846

Six Words from
Senator Daniel Webster of Massachusetts
in Opposition to the War with Mexico

You have a Sparta.
Embellish it!

March 1846

Found on the Composing Room Floor
of the New York *Sun*

Dispatch to Mr. Moses Beach, Publisher, from his reporter travelling to join
General Taylor on the Río Nueces

If you should come to me
And there and then
Should pay me out

I'd shout:
"I shall arise again!
I shall resurrect!"

Oh, happy, happy me!
But knowing you, you'll stop your check,
And I'll drop dead again!

This is my final notice!

S. L. C.
March 1846

Mrs. Anne Royall's Pen Portrait of General Sam Houston, Senator from the New State of Texas

You will note the Senator stands six feet four.
He wears a modest suit of gray, embroidered
in black braid. A flaming red *serape* blanket
hangs across his shoulders, giving him the air
of Conqueror.

When presented to a lady, he first takes one
step forward, bows very low, and says, "Lady,
I salute you." All this performed with the several
shows and flourishes of a Spanish fencing lesson.
The *General Houston greeting* now reigns as fashion.
Democrats, Locofocos, Massachusetts Whigs take note!

Anne Royall, Editor
The Huntress
Washington, D.C.
March 1846

Work

Lowell, Massachusetts. Seven thousand girls
walk silently along its streets. Half dark. Patches
of snow and mud. Dawn to dark at the looms,
three bits a day.

A petition goes from hand
to hand to cut the workday hours from fourteen
down to ten.

◆ ◆

Then there is Mister Howe,
inventor of a new machine replete with slots
and tensions, headpieces and spirals, cogs and cylinders.
It can sew the seam of a pair of pantaloons from cuff
to hip in three minutes flat.

Think of the seamstresses!

◆ ◆

Richmond, Virginia. A gang of slaves converts
tobacco leaves to cakes of *Honeydew,*
"the chewing man's choice." Their overseers ensure
they make no sound. Not a word. Nothing.

When the slaves are let go at night, they sing—solos,
duets, and glees.

◆ ◆

In Washington, a senator laughs, "I have so much
to do today I think I'll go home to bed!"

March 1846

From a Letter Written by
Captain John Charles Frémont to His Wife
Regarding His Explorations of California

Jess, I'm Fortune's darling. I find a summit
in an unknown mountain range, I plant my banner
in the midst of raging storms—I'm the one
for storms, they whet my appetite for getting to the top!

Here I've fixed another banner high
upon a summit. Thirteen stripes, a corner
field of white, a blue eagle perched atop
a peace pipe, surrounded by blue stars. The emblem of a summit
and a vision, Jess. It's from this peak I see
a shining web—the tarns and lakes, the streams
and headwaters, of the mighty Colorado River. And beyond,
the distant Wind River that feeds the Yellowstone
and then runs eastward, on to the Missouri. I see
a continent, ready and ripe for winning! And the flag
is my sign, my emblem—the peace pipe, stars, and eagle.

Suddenly it comes over me—I'm back in 1838,
I'm out among the Dakotas at Pipestone Quarry. I find
that I can leap off a bluff across the intervening
space and land on a pedestal of rock whose top
is barely one foot square. You wrote me then
such exploits show a hardihood that even those
who puff and vaunt that they are mountain men
never do possess. I do, I know I do.
That is the hardest thing for others to accept.

The wild, Jess. Once you've been in the clouds, with the sun
blazing on everlasting glaciers—and the peaks beyond
so solemn, still, austere—the world below
is a petty sort of place. The noblest work
of nature is the wild. The free. The untrammelled. All
my heart is there. And will be, all my life.

March 1846

Dispatch to General Ampudia
in Mexico City

From General José Mariano Arista at Matamoros

*Me permitad de elevar a Vuestra presencia el acontecimiento de los hechos
recientes en territorio nacional al borde del Río Grande del Norte.*

A force of sixty-three dragoons, armed,
belligerent, and carrying the Northamerican flag
violated Mexican soil today. Behind them
General Taylor's army builds a stronghold,
one they call Fort Texas.

                Our spies inform us
General Taylor wishes that *the war with Mexico*
(he does not hesitate to use the term)
were at an end. He fears his nation's appetite
for land. That it comes at the expense of what he terms
a weak power. That someday they will prove to be quite
powerless to carry out their schemes in the vastness
of our territories.

                General Taylor does not wish
to be a pawn in the schemes of President Polk.
Or scapegoat, either, when all goes awry. Polk plots
and plots—the Texas revolt, inciting our Indians
to rebel, incursions into California—he eats us, piecemeal!

As for his officers, they lack in zeal. Many
of their troops are foreigners. They do not shoot or ride
or even manage horses well. But eat? Yes,

they do that well—wagon trains, full of food!
As to the dragoons: we left sixteen dead
and many wounded. The survivors are our prisoners.

Their army? Three thousand men, not more. What
can an enemy do with a force so small?

                     They have made
their move. Now we may say: *hostilities have begun.*

April 24, 1846

A Second Note from an
Adviser to the President

Events, sir—you must beware of them! In this rude excuse
for a democracy they can be your fondest friend or your most
malicious enemy. Recall that General Washington
once described the populace as nothing more
than a ruminating herd, ranging over millions
of miles of virgin land, slaughtering the game
and killing off indigenous tribes so as to set
their plowshares deep in wondrous fertile soil.

Keep them at it and everything goes swimmingly
for us. But let one adverse word come back
(seven weeks in transit, with another week
for us to frame a suitable response, which then
must tediously return the route) and four long months
will pass. Doubt sets in among the populace
like gangrene.

        Plan until you are blue in the face,
things just happen. Look at the map. Our English
cousins seek to box us in: Canada
to our north; Oregon; then Florida and the Indies to our south.
Most recently their purpose is to pit the Mexicans
against us all the way from Texas to the Californias.
By this last, we are surrounded!

        One day
our ruminating herd will ram against a point
of no return. Bitter encounters with alien

flags and troops will goad their lust for land
to fury. The British know full well the herd
will undergo a metamorphosis of mood from pastoral
to ugly. They know that it will promptly turn
on us. We will be the ones to feel its wrath!

The fault? All ours! Every blighted hope
will come to be a course in a journalistic feast
served up daily in the penny press. This must not
be. Sir, it is we who must control events!

April 1846

Scrap of President Polk's Notes
for His War Message to Congress

California / California / *California*
Slidell? / Stockton? / Fremont?
?

The bitter cup of Mexican
The cup of our forbearance
The cup of our forbearance had been exhausted

Menaces / Invasion
Frontier / Rio del Norte (Grande)
even before the recent information from our frontier.

              Matamoros / Taylor? / Whigs?
Mexico vs. U.S.
But now, after reiterated menaces, Mexico has passed

Texas / Alamo / 28th state
Texas border claim
the boundary of the United States, has invaded our territory

Our claim
U.S. troops / U.S. soil
and shed American blood upon American soil.

Hostilities = Act of War = Declaration of war
In doing so, she has proclaimed that hostilities have commenced

Clarify:
De facto
and the two nations are now at war. As war exists,

Not our wish
Settle outstanding U.S. claims / Solve peacefully
notwithstanding all our efforts to avoid it,

Restate / Mexico's doing
Matter of honor / Respond to challenge
and exists by the act of Mexico herself, we are called upon

Patriotism / Nation among nations
Show British / Show Europeans
by every consideration of duty and patriotism to vindicate

Election of 1848 / Remove Whig threat
California
with decision the honor, the rights, and the interests of our
    country . . .

May 1846

Statement by
Albert Gallatin on the
Declaration of War with Mexico

I believe in this Republic. I stood with Thomas
Jefferson, General Washington, Mister Hamilton.
Young I may have been, but I was Swiss, and they knew
I knew banking. I have served the Republic ever since.

Now I am old and no more inclined to lengthy
argument. Simply put, this Mexican War
is pure aggression. In private life the President
would never dare appropriate his neighbor's farm
on such pretenses as he would use today to tear
the Mexican Republic limb from limb.

                        How
can this be? The ruling party now asserts
that we Americans possess some great superiority
stemming from our "race." It dominates all else. I ask,
what effort or dedication or faith is needed to believe
in the superiority of a race? Imagine the lassitude, the sloth,
the corruption that springs from cherishing such a notion!
This dream of race is not the dream of a true
Republic. And yet they speak of Empire, of dominion—
of the whole continent subjected to our will through the universal
monarchy of our race!

                      There is no restraint in their thinking,
if thinking it is. It lays bare their greed. Their merciless
ambition. Their vanity.

Our mission as a republic is precisely this:
to show superiority of race does not exist.

May 1846

Triumph of Our Troops at
Palo Alto and Resaca de la Palma

Dispatch to the New York *Sun*

*From our reporter travelling with General Taylor in Mexico—dispatch
service by our packet boat, direct*

"God has deserted the Mexican soldier." So say
the Mexicans themselves! In but a weekend's time
our force three thousand strong has overcome
the flower of Mexico's finest. We faced a multitude,
tens of thousands of dragoons, artillery, and infantry.
Result: The Mexicans lost five hundred men.
Our losses were but *four!* And wounded, forty-two.

This message goes by courier, thence to the packet
boat for Baltimore, so brevity must be the rule.
We ask, What happened to the Mexicans? They meant to fight
and fought they did, but our soldiers say their guns
refused to fire, their cannonballs fell short
or rolled like bowling balls along the ground.
Mexicans—blame not God, but your stand of arms!

S. L. C.
May 1846

A Dinner at the White House

Paté de fois gras and garnished ham, croquettes
and oyster pie, canvasback duck and turkey,
côtelettes de mouton, snowball potatoes and peas,
oranges, sweetmeats, ices, prunes

                              and wines
in alternating colors: pink champagne, ruby
port, amber Madeira, pale green Rhine,
yellow sauterne, and golden sherry

                             served
on gold-band plates with crests in blue and goblets
of blue cut glass

                    with flowers and silver candelabra
laid on mirrors trimmed with vines that catch
the light from crystal chandeliers

                         and window drapes
of gold and purple velvet

                    and the chairs of carved
and polished rosewood, with purple velvet seats

and on the walls—mirrors, mirrors, more mirrors.

                                      June 1846

A Defection

To the Editor of the *Pennsylvania Freeman:*

Can it be there lives so flagrant a fool? I refer
to the eminent Mister Cassius Clay, unswerving
opponent of slavery in any form, archenemy
of Texas statehood, tireless advocate of education
and the arts—the man who faced down mobs that panted
for his life with rifles, shotguns, Mexican cavalry
lances, and two brass cannons. He has changed his tune!

Once the war with Mexico was "degrading both
to the government that would consummate it, and degrading to
        the people that submit to it."

Now he says, "War exists!
Resistance to it now would be rebellion.
The war that once seemed wicked and unjust should now
be pressed with vigor."

                    Mister Emerson
has said: "There is a certain satisfaction
in coming down to the lowest ground in politics.
We get rid thereby of hypocrisy and cant."

Now may we say, "We know the real man!"

June 1846

A Share in the Underground Railroad

Husband and wife they are. But slaves. They live
across the river in Kentucky, not quite a dozen
miles from Cincinnati. Very valuable
property, too—and for that, their master would sell them
down the river. They run away, and come

to Levi Coffin. Four hundred dollars is the sum
their master bids to bring them back in chains.
Quaker Levi hides them in his garret
but Canada is far away. Money for a carriage
and a team is what he does not have. So out

he goes one morning to collect. He asks a merchant,
"Does Thee own stock in the Underground Railroad?" "What road
is that?" "The one on which we send the fugitive
slaves to Canada." "If that's the road, I own a
little stock in it." "Well then, the stock has been
assessed, and I'm the one who's authorized to collect."
"How much?" "Mine was a dollar, and I suppose that thine
will be the same." The merchant smiles and gives
a dollar. Quaker Levi goes next door
to a store whose keeper is a Jew. Once told just how
the money would be used, he subscribes two dollars. And so
it goes—the druggist, the queensware dealer, down
to the wholesale grocer. Levi knows the owner
is not in sympathy but asks him anyway.
"Friend, does Thee own stock in the Underground Railroad?"
"No!" is the grocer's cry. "Why, it pays well!
Thee ought to take some stock—it makes one feel

so good, especially when he's called on for assessments."
"I don't believe in helping fugitives, and there's
an end to it!" Levi smiles: "Good Friend, I don't
believe Thee knows what Thee is saying. Suppose
thy wife were captured and carried off by Indians
or Algerines and suffered all the cruelties and hardships
that a slave endures. Then she escapes, barefoot,
bareheaded, with but a little clothing. She must perish
without some aid or be recaptured and sold
into slavery once again. Now suppose
that someone comes to take an interest in her behalf
and calls on me to help in gaining her
her freedom. And I refuse to do it, saying,
'I don't believe in helping fugitives. And there's
an end to it!' What would Thee think of me?" "I don't
expect my wife to ever be in such
conditions." "I pray she will not be," says Levi.
"But I know of someone's wife who is. My conscience
calls for me to help. It always does me
good to help. And I am never one
to relish one good thing without a wish
for others to partake in it. So it is
I thought to give Thee this one chance." He tells him
then of the man and wife who would be sold
down river, how they escaped bareheaded, barefoot,
and thinly clad, hastening across the water
to Ohio. "Great exertions are being made to drag them
back to slavery. I ask Thee, take stock. Help us
clothe and send these people on to Canada.
I know that Thee would feel the better, giving
something for their relief. Now I have done
my duty, I've given Thee the chance to give.
If Thee is not disposed, 'tis thine own look-out,

not mine." Levi leaves him then. Coming
by the store again, the merchant calls
him over. "I'll give you a trifle. Nothing more."
He subscribes a half a dollar. Says
Levi, "Now I'm sure that Thee'll feel better."
One week later, Levi sees him standing
in the street. "Did they get off safely?" asks the grocer
in a whisper. Levi laughs. "Thee hast taken
stock in the Underground Railroad. Thee feels an interest
in it. Had Thee not taken stock, Thee would care
nothing for them. Yes, they got off safely!
By now they'll be in Canada." Then Levi sells
another share of stock. And the two men part as friends.

July 1846

Mister Frederick Douglass Writes
from England

"Persecuted, hunted, outraged in America, I have come
to England. Behold the change: the chattel becomes
a man, and I am free!

            All is so different
here. Color is no barrier to equality.
No prejudice to feel, no insults to encounter. All
is smooth. Imagine—to be treated as a man and brother!"

◆ ◆

"I hear that Captain Frémont has raised his flag
in California. He claims it as a new Republic. His flag
is simple, one of unbleached cloth, adorned
with a grizzly bear that faces one red star.
The conqueror of California! The antislavery cause
supreme, the crime of Texas compensated! May he govern
well. May he bring his newborn nation into
the Union and become its Senator, to offset Houston.
And may he be our nation's President someday!"

July 1846

Mister Adams Takes a Swim

Summer is upon us. The octogenarian Mister
Adams, beloved former president now representing
Massachusetts in the House, has taken to Potomac
waters once again—his favorite swimming
hole behind the White House. We honor this salutary
custom. His labors to thwart a war with Mexico
exhausted him.
                    Let it also be said the eminent Mister
Adams stood firm against the huntress of the *The Huntress*
who importuned him for an interview. The woman
stood upon the presidential clothes while he
engaged in his matutinal natation. Naked came he
into the world, and naked must he needs emerge
unless he granted her that interview!

> *National Intelligencer*
> Washington, D.C.
> July 1846

James Beckwourth, Mountain Man, and the Bounty Hunters

"You can swear, you can pray. Whatever you do, jest keep
it to yourself. Say nothin', do less, that's
the ticket. If you see a man's mule that's runnin' off,
don't stop it. Let 'er go to the devil, t'ain't one
of yours. If his possible sack falls off, don't tell him.
He'll find it out hisself. At camp, help cook,
get wood and water. Look smart. Get your pipe
an' smoke it. Don't ask too many questions an' you'll pass.

"You bet my mother war a slave. I got a 1800
silver dollar on a rawhide round my neck.
That's fer when I war born. My freedom papers?
Signed by my daddy, long gone. But don't you try
to mess with me. This child ain't got his moccasins
on fer nothin', that's a fact! A dozen
years I camped with Crows. I'm *The Antelope,*
Bull's Robe, The Enemy of Horses, Bloody Arm,
ecsetry. I'm black, I'm Injun by choice, an' proud
of both!

     "It war on the Missouri. Kit Carson an' I
war takin' a wagon train across the river.
I war standin' guard on the cavyard while Kit went out
to hunt. A pair of bounty hunters an' their dawgs
come rushin' from the M'ssouri side. I put up
some fight, but it war two to one. They put the handcuffs
on an' tole me I war a damn nigger
an' I'd run away an' they had cotched me.

"Wall, I am one lucky hoss. Jest then
Kit Carson's men rode in an' ordered them
to stop. Up come the guns. The M'ssourians said
they'd take this nigger, the Carson men said no,
it war four to two. Off come the handcuffs
an' the minute I war free I grabbed a gun an' shot
the dawgs. Prize bloodhounds, both. That got right to 'em
so one took aim on me an' fired. An' missed.
They turned an' ran. One shot from me an' I killt
the one. Then I killt the other.
                              "That got
the U.S. marshal on my trail. But only fer a week.
After all, the bounty hunters got
what they deserved. An' I war on my way
to Santy Fe to do a piece of service
fer the U.S. Army. Nice country there, good
place to put a inn for trav'lers. Enterprise,
an' all. An' I got friends along the way
I want to see. Ho fer the mountings, boys!"

August 1846

Margaret Fuller's Notes on Her
Voyage to Europe

ITEM: Miss Margaret Fuller, well-known to thoughtful Americans as the Literary Editress of Mister R. W. Emerson's late quarterly magazine, The Dial, has sailed for Europe. She has been commissioned by this newspaper to send back regular dispatches regarding the latest developments in thought, government and the arts.

Horace Greeley, Editor
New York Tribune

Mister Emerson must be taken for what he is,
as he wishes to be taken. Younger, I liked to be
in his library when he was not there. It seemed
a sacred place. So much soul was there
I did not need a book. He lived in his own way,
and I never kept him from his duties any more
than would a book. He did not soothe the illness
or the morbid feelings of his friends because he did
not wish that anybody do it for him.

He was true to himself.

We worked.

But Boston! What could it be to me?
What could it be but a ghostlike home? No,
no home at all. There in New England there is no such
thing as flesh and blood, you only hob-a-nob
with spirits. You love nothing, you criticize everything—the very
atmosphere is critical, with every twig defined
intensely in a sky so hard, so distant.

♦ ♦

And the men,
remember the men! One, unforgettably. Poised
above the torrent at Niagara, gazing down at it.
Then calmly, reflectively he spits in a long descending
arc, down into the tumult.

And father. A thinking
man, a lawyer. But mostly and forever, a businessman.
And oh, the spirit of utility! From my tenderest years
he hoped to make me heir to all he knew—
mathematics, history, geography, Latin. But
his habits, plus his hopeless, cold ambition for a daughter
who could only be a nothing in the world of men,
had made him hard. He deprived me of my childhood
and on my youthful sensibility he spread nightmares, spectres,
congestion of the brain. Somnambulism,
everlasting headaches. I suffered all of them.

♦ ♦

Nothing now, but sea. Water, horizon to horizon.
A prospect of indifference to everyone and everything.
To New Englanders who pray and find that they
are talking to themselves. To their tragic concern and tragic
exaltation. To their misery and earnest self-importance.

To them I cry, "Occasionally one must be unworthy!
Simply to be able to go on living one must
prove to be unworthy. Only then
may one be worthy of beauty, art, and thought."

♦ ♦

Oh, give me truth! Cheat me by no illusion!

August 1846

The Angel of the Prairies

dear Cousin Kate

you will never guess what happened
you remember Ray Ennersly that second boy of Jack's
the one what seemed like he was never going
anywheres but down, well, he held forth
at the big camp meeting, he had a vision and words
in his mouth were nothing like him thank the Lord for that
if they were nobody would of believed him but there
he was and it was something and they got a paper
and wrote it down, you study it and let me know
what do you think and that's what everybody is talking
about and did he ever have any fainting spells

Your loving cousin Elspeth

♦ ♦ ♦ ♦

To Christians Everywhere!

The Angel of the Prairies appeared to me. He was of a mild
intelligent countenance. In his hand was a curious glass
and looking into it I beheld the fate of Empires
and the destiny of nations. Here is what I saw:
America, yea, the continent ever destined
for the seat of Empire, here shall the ambassadors of all nations
resort with tributes to the Master Nation, and it will be greater
than the Persia of Cyrus!

The seat of all Empires began
East of Eden and it has ever since been westering.
It came down on the plains of the Euphrates under Nimrod,
Nebuchadnezzar, Cyrus, and Alexander. It rested
for a time, then took to westering again. It took
its seat in Palestine, and finally on the banks of the Nile.

After a while it penetrated to the British Isles.
It sojourned for a spell, preparing for a voyage. Sent
advance guards out to make a way in the wilderness,
passed over the great Atlantic waters, and it was us
Americans who finally founded a government on this continent.

Said the Angel:
The capital of the world will never be
on the Atlantic shore, I say it will come to be
in the middle of the continent! Iowa and Wisconsin will come
to have a hundred million, Texas and all
of Mexico will repose in the bosom of these United

States. No less than two hundred million citizens
therein!

And the Angel of the Prairies continued unto me,
Ray Ennersly: *Internal corruption and contention have ever*
been grievous in man's affairs. But in wilderness America
a noble form of government shall be set up, yea,
the good the great and patriotic will unto it repair.
This government will be no human Monarchy. Nor will it
be Democracy. They have oppressed the humble
workingmen and trod upon the widow and the orphan.
No, the great new government of the West will have God
HimSelf as head, yea, all honor to the great God

Elohim, He shall rule with a council called the Ancient
of Days. Under the constant direction of the Almighty
HimSelf.

Said the Angel: *Oh my people! Listen
to what I say and do likewise. Abolish the cruel
custom of prisons, abolish the penitentiaries,
abolish the court-martials for desertion. Let peace and friendship
reign over all! Yea, when the prisons be opened
the eyes and ears and hearts of the people will be opened
also. They will behold true freedom!*
The Angel ended thus: *All men shall be
free agents. As much in the temples of commerce or the courts
of law or the Great Temple of the Holy of Holies, all men
shall be free agents.*

This is what the Angel
of the Prairies revealed to me, Ray Ennersly,
His servant. May His name be praised forever! Selah!

*Persons wishing to know more about this revelation are invited to write to
Brother Ray Ennersly, c/o General Delivery, Antlers, Arkansas.*

August 1846

President Polk, in Charge,
and the Capture of Monterey

This war will not be like our last one.

♦ ♦

                    The war
against the British. Madison, the schoolmaster. He thought
his underlings would do their duty. They merely
did what they wished.

♦ ♦

               This war will be run from the Oval
Office. It will be run from my desk. Absolute control.

♦ ♦

There are great embarrassments. How to control
the movements of our forces when we have no maps
that are reliable. No inventory of supplies that might
be drawn from the countryside. Nothing, except what spies
may tell us. Or may not. All chance.

♦ ♦

                  And General Taylor.
From Mexico he gives the smallest quantity
of information. He has the mien of a regular
soldier, waiting to obey my orders. He gives
no sign of a grasp of mind that is suited to his position.

♦ ♦

He is obdurate. Avoids all responsibility. Makes
no suggestions, gives no opinions.

♦ ♦

                 He is a Whig
Surely his eyes are turned toward the next election.

Replace him. Why not my law partner, Gideon Pillow?
Name him general, take his place. Loyalty.

◆ ◆ ◆ ◆

Added, in Polk's hand:

The packet boat brings news: MONTEREY IS OURS!
The city fell in just four days! How
Why wasn't I informed?

What will I do with the man? He is twice a hero!

Will Congress strike a second gold medallion
in his likeness?
                    This afternoon —Meet with cabinet!

James K. Polk, *Diary*
September 1846

Seb Simon, Volunteer, U.S. Army, Explains
Some Regional Differences

Those Massachusetts fellas, they're so dim
they can't see shit in a snowbank. And those Show-Mes from
    Missouri—
they're a chapter in themselves! It wasn't a month ago
I heard their senator was writin' up a book,
"Thirty Years in the United States Senate,
or, A History of the Working of the American Government."
Well, since there's a outside as well as inside
to everything, and since "some things can be done as well as
    others,"
I'm hereby givin' out my book—*"My Thirty*
Years Out of the Senate, or, A History of Me and My
Ancestral Posterity, in Its Entirety!"
                              I got
to be a major in this war with Mexico. Even
as a pup I was the one for headwork—back then,
to gain the name of scholar. How? I'd take ·
a great big apple every day to school
and give it to my cousin Obadiah if he'd sit
behind me. He was a proud fierce reader, and when I'd come
to a word I didn't know he'd just lean over
and whisper it to me. Then I'd read it loud
and proper.
             One day I come to a great long crooked
word I couldn't git the meat of. He whispers
"Skip it!" The moment I hear him, I bawl out, "Skip it!"
"Eh? What's that?" cries out the master. I look
again. Obie chokes, then pokes me. "Skip it!"

says I. The master looks as if he's caught
a weasel fast asleep. He gives me one big
yaw-haw right in my face. Right then I drops
the book and streak it, I mean, I pull both feet
for home and never show my face in school
again.

Which is the origin, as you might say,
of another book. I'm writin' it, it's titled *"My Thirty
Years Out of School—And Out of the Senate—by a Maine
Downeaster, Hero of the Battle at Monterey"!*

September 1846

To the Nations of Europe Concerning
Our War with Mexico, and the
Capture of Monterey

O Europe, reflect—we are a new nation! We are unlike
your principalities and powers—freedom has bestowed uncounted
blessings on this land. The eagle on our coin flies surely
in the winds of commerce. We are possessed by fervor, we are
    certain
of our right. And we shall boldly go through fire and water
to win the uncharted vastness of our Western Commonwealth!
Hand in hand with this, behold, there has supervened
a great awakening, a vast unforced outpouring
of fervor, piety and Christian zeal. A Millennium
is being shown to us to contemplate. It is a time for visions,
a time to speak in tongues.
                        There are those who scoff
at this. They say our great awakening is mere
convenience, that it gilds our lust for a Western Wilderness.
We reply: your average American is a straightforward sort
of person. His sorrows and his joys are deeply felt
and celebrated openly. What can he feel but joy
when the Texans' revolt from Mexico results in triumph?
Jacksonian democracy and the Protestant faith, victorious!

The Texans have voted freely now to join
the Union. We both are making common cause
against the Mexicans. Unhappy Mexico, weighted
down by centuries of cruelty, idolatry, misrule.
Let them hear the clarion call: we fight for the triumph
of truth and righteousness!

Who would presume to damp
the fires that drive our westward movement? We say to them:
we are entering a Millennium, but we need not die, or take on
new flesh. Providence decrees that we shall consummate
everything, now, in this world, in our own flesh. Ours
will be a commonwealth far more bountiful than any
ever seen. And we shall be a nation
far more just, far more enduring than the one
descried by Abraham, Father of all Nations!

United States Magazine and Democratic Review
September 1846

Mister Morse's Machine

makes the wires talk. Went down by the War Department,
paid two bits. Clickety-clack. The clerk
comes up and grins. *It is a fine day* is what he's written
on a paper. That is what it said, he says.
Well, clickety-clack says I, I know damn well
the day is fine. And I am two bits lighter
and you are two bits heavier. Just what's the point?
He says, Right now, I can repeat this message
to New York, New Haven, Philadelphia, Boston—
And Timbuctoo, for all I care! says I.
What the hell do they care to know about
our weather? Says he, That's not the point. Give us
a year and we'll be sending to Saint Louis. Says I,
At six bits a word, I guess! Says he, You guessed
it right. Says I, And *that* will be one fine
clickety-clack for you—and Mister Morse!
It is a fine day, says he. *A very fine day!*

September 1846

A Clarification from the Editor of the
United States Magazine and
Democratic Review

"Manifest Destiny"

We were the ones who coined the phrase. It was meant
to be a byword. One that would mark our place
at the table of nations. One to make clear we take
exception to the plots devised by Spain and Britain
to baffle our expansion. They have conspired to foil our policies,
to hamstring our national powers. They would thwart the
reason
for our nation's life and breath—to colonize the continent
consigned to us by Providence!
Yet some object. They ask:
is *slavery* "manifest" in our manifest destiny? We tell them:
slavery has no part in it, it is indigenous to the South and slaves
will inevitably be drawn off there. And what of *Texas*?
We say: its annexation was inevitable, by force of arms, or not.
It is westward, ever westward that our people move.
It is ordained to be so. California soon will be
enfolded in our flag. The Anglo-Saxon foot
already treads its limits. An irresistible army
of pioneers pours down upon it, their only arms
the plow and rifle. But this is an army that leaves
not carnage in its wake but the fruits of progress: schools
and colleges, courts and congresses, mines and meeting houses.
Three hundred million of us, Americans all,
are destined to dwell upon this continent.

And all shall gather under the Stars and Stripes in a fast-hastening year!

That is the meaning of *Manifest Destiny!*

September 1846

An Advisory to the President from Doctor Josiah C. Nott, Noted Physician and Ethnologist, of Mobile, Alabama, on the Subject of the Mexican Race

Now, as to the various Indian families of the Americas,
North, Central, and South—one group has put up
monuments, another is made up of wandering tribes,
etcetera.

       What is the real worth of any of them?
The beaver and the bee display the very skills
in building monuments as do the Mexicans. In fact,
everything in the history of the bee will show a reasoning
power little short of theirs. I have concluded
that the Indian—North or South American or Mexican—
is not an improvable breed.

                Note, however,
that even in the supreme expression of humanity, the Caucasian
race, there are gradations. The ancient German
is the parent stock from which our highest modern
civilizations sprang. The finest blood of France
and England is the German. The ruling caste in Russia
is the German. Look at the United States, then contrast
our virile people with the dark-skinned Spaniards to the south.

You will see for yourself. It is unnecessary to draw conclusions.

October 1846

A Letter to President James K. Polk from an Overseer of His Plantation

Dear Sir:

I once more will endeaver to write to you
a fiew lines that you may hear from us   with regard to adderson and
gilburt they got to here a few weaks since
then gilburt left about a weak along
hea got away to tennessee   he stade three days
they sent him back in irons   when he got to here
hea stade two nights and left again without
one lik or short word what ware not don according
to your request   I should of whip him soon
as he landed had it not bin of your request
that mr bobit should be present tho I think
if I had taken him and whip him soon as he got

to hear he would not of run away again
which I would of dun but I thought you would of thought
that I would whup him overmuch though that
is what I never dun since I been dooing
binness and it is what I would not doo to disenable
them from work one our   my fealings would not
suffer mea to gone as fair as that

                              I will say
to you what I jest learnt from the negrows   gilbert
says that doctor Caldwell wantes to buy him
and I expec that hea is gone back to him
again but do not sell him if you wish to brake him

running off for they had just as lief be sold
twice than bea whip once   they kno you are
the presydent and I beleave that they beleave
tennessee is a place of parradise and they all want
to gow up there so stop them   put them in irons
when they sent back and soon they wil stop ther cumming
to tennessee

        I no that you aire very much
perplext about your negrows running off
you wil finde that you wil have to bea the man
and put a stop to that   I think that you
must faul upon a plan and brake them   if you will keep
it up for a time or two then they will brake

I have got my handsful to save the crop and I
am livving hear for small wages   I shall ask you $500
for next year   you will want sum plowes on the farm
for another year and I think it best to get them
up in Memphis   it will take a half a dozen
one horse plows

                Yours respectfully,
                Isaac H. Dismukes

Beanland Plantation
Fayette, Mississippi

                      October 1846

From the Notebook of
Ralph Waldo Emerson

I bitterly opposed the annexation of Texas. And now
we have a war with Mexico. The balance of free
and slave forever will be altered in the scales of this
republic.
        Headlong annexations to this country bring us
ill effects and bitter moral issues.
But I am not prepared to censure out-
of-hand the innate drive to dominate
our English race embodies.

        We have a singleness
of heart that contrasts with the Latin races. We conquer
with our head as well as with our hands. Americans
possess an inner, vital force—our English
forebears bequeathed to us a primal energy.
Races need such energy if they are not
to be destroyed.

        It is a peculiarity of our history
that there may be materialism, there may be
vulgarity, there may be lust for land. But always
and forever, there will burn a flame of longing. And what
is it for? For individual freedom. It redeems
our excesses, no matter how unthinking!

October 1846

A Translation from the
Notebook of Professor Louis Agassiz,
the Swiss Naturalist

His Arrival in the United States

I have always believed in the specific unity of man. And why? Because man alone among all organized beings—plants as well as animals—is spread over the entire surface of the earth. It is as simple as that.

But now I have come to America, to the city of Philadelphia. I have come to this city because I have heard so much about its scientists and the collections to be found in its museums, and I said to myself, I must observe it all!

I have been so impressed by what is called here the Academy of Natural Sciences that I have hardly left the building during my stay. *Que magnifique!* Six hundred Indian skulls, of all the tribes who now inhabit or formerly inhabited the continent of North America. Nothing like it exists anywhere else. This one collection alone is worth my journey to America.

But this ethnological Golgotha is nothing when compared to the effect which has been made on me by the living specimens of humankind who wait on my table in my hotel here in Philadelphia. *Les negres.* I had never seen a black man before; it is obvious that they are unknown in my native Switzerland. *Mais ces couleur!* A purple black! And their peculiar limbs and hands. And their large lips and their black heads topped with wool, instead of hair—*quelle fascination!* Fascination, yes—and disgust. I stared at them, I stared most discourteously, and when one of them, a certain waiter, approached, it was all I could do to keep from bolting from the room.

I said to myself, *mon cher Louis,* that specimen is human? Yes, I answered, recalling my belief in the specific unity of man. He is a human being. But is this creature of the same species as me, a white man? I asked myself.

Later, I asked this very question of my American hosts. Oh yes, they said, the blacks, it is a very sad affair, anyone can see that they are not the equal of whites, even the abolitionists who work so hard to free them say the same. And, my hosts went on, even when they are free, the Negroes are excluded from society by the force of an instinctive repugnance. Even the ultras among the society of the abolitionists, no matter how sympathetic their views to the plight of the Negroes, would not allow their daughters to have anything to do with them.

Agassiz, now it is clear that one can no longer harmonize geology with Genesis! Those people are not the descendants of Noah. They have come from other ancestors. It is surely a notion without the slightest scientific basis to assume that all living human beings derive from one common center of origin!

No. Plants, animals, and human beings were first created in several parts of the world—and only within those districts where they would naturally be capable of inhabiting for a certain time.

And now it occurs to me—it is a *coup de tête*—that animals, all animals including mankind, were not created in pairs. Yes, it is natural for some animals to live in pairs, but whoever has heard of a pair of herrings? Or a pair of buffaloes? Or a pair of bees? I am much too good a naturalist, too much accustomed by now to differentiate between the animals, to accept the unity of conception of the genus *Homo*. No, there could not have been a single creation. No, no, no! Multiple creations.

And God? Always there must be a God. If He did not exist, one would have to posit him. So the divisions of the animal kingdom may originally have been thoughts in the mind of that Creator. Each animal species would be a manifestation of a special thought; each animal family a combination of similar thoughts; every great division of the animal kingdom a particular train of reflection upon a fundamental idea.

Whatever the end of all this may be, it spells the end of Genesis. The philosophy of science obliges us to look these matters in the face. Any other course would be mock-philanthropy and mock-science. I have seen the beginning of a new age! And it is all because of these waiters.

October 1846

Harriet Beecher Stowe

surveyed the color-scheme of children
in her husband Calvin's school. Here

were white and black and mixed-race, shoulder
to shoulder, tongues-in-teeth, heads bent,

writing at their desks. Mister Macrae,
her guest, was asking how the different

races did—"And what, indeed,
of the future of the Negro race?"

                              "The future
is quite good," replied the authoress, "and I am very
hopeful. Black children get on just
as fast as whites. But the mixed race ones
are weaker." "You ask of the mixed race children?"

Calvin echoed. "They are sure to die out soon."

November 1846

A Report from the
Volunteer Training Camps

Lud Jessup and His Lizards

"Tell your troubles to Jesus—'cause there ain't
no chaplains here!" That would be the way of it
after Corpus Christi. Not one Bible
or blackcoat minister to be seen. Not like the other
war, where we got to whale the British and
get prayed on while we did. This war is goin'
to be straight-out and gen-u-ine, 'pon
my nonner, nothin' but!

                        Yaw, but there's
always a colonel's wife what thinks we got
a need for the Holy Spirit. So into our pillar
of dust by day there rides old Parson Buller
on a mule. He had the face and the humor for stompin'
out vice and sin, wherever. And did he have
a voice! Stand at the bottom of Niagry Falls,
try spittin' up into it! Stay close to home,
put yourself in front of a cyclone, try
callin' your dog! With Buller nigh the lugs
on the head of sin would stand out clear as ticks
on a new-sheared sheep. Soon as he arrived
there was a dillberry reek of brimstone on the wind
and you could see blue flames was lickin' out
of tunics and canteens. And kit bags, with their decks of cards!
Me? You bet Lud Jessup's a bettin' man.
See that gopher over there. I'll bet

he wiggles that nose of his six times afore
he blinks—money on the table! As for Buller, I thinks,
what would it take to set that preachin' hurricane
ninety degrees off course? Quite a bit!
says my wagerin' self, say, ten-to-one. I mean
the feller's one hard biscuit! And he's prone to launch
himself on tangents—rum and 'bacca—and like
to spoutin' poetry like

> Them who smoke Havannies
> All get a foul disease!
> They get brainless as chimpanzees,
>   They get meagre as lizards!
> They go mad, they beat their wives!
> They lead awful sinful lives!
> They plunge carvin' knives
>   Into their gizzards!

etcetera. So I goes prepared. I'm first in line,
and I'm headin' for the mourners' bench like I was one
big canoodler. No trick in that. It's worse than true!

The meetin' was a dandyfunk. Buller went off like a rocket,
nothin' less. It's not more than a hour till he gets
to rum and 'bacca and blue fire and brimstone.
And his lizards. Well, what do I have in my knapsack
but a nice collection—six or seven of them cuddlers.
Regardin' lizards, Texas is the place to take
the cork right outten the bottle—they's long spikey fellas
with tongues come flickin' out and droopy eyes
and diamond backs.

Buller now is rollin'
down the high slopes of his preachin', how the lizards of hell
are apt to coil up in your bedrolls in the night, how the oldest
and worst will crawl right into your boots and up your legs
and under your drawers, no odds how tight you tie them.
You could hear grown men begin to fret. They'd cry,
"Oh no! Not my drawers!" and it was turnin' into
a mighty draggle—the boys a-shiftin' and yippin'—
good boys they were, right off the farm—but all
that talk of lizards crawlin' on their skin and the nip
and nibble of awful sin was turnin' them distract!

Buller is standin' on a bench and holdin' forth
like a four-deck steamboat toilin' up the Mississippi.
He's sawin' his arms, recitin' "foul disease"
at the colonel's wife. Right then is when I unties
my knapsack and lets my lizards loose. It's as if
them little scamps had known just where good nestin'
was, I mean, all of them scooted out
of my sack like *shoosh* and underneath his pantslegs quick
as a fuse of gunpowder burns on a August day,
and makin' a noise like squirrels racin' up
a shellbark hickory tree. Buller is right
in the middle of

They go mad, they beat their wives!
They lead awful sinful lives!—

when he comes full stop. He looks for a moment like a old sow
does when she hears you whistlin' for the dogs. He's just
hangin'

there on the "sin" in sinful when one of my lizards
pokes his head right out from under his collar!
Then you see ripples movin' inside his pants.
He gets this look of sufferin' on his face,
the kind a man will feel but can't do nothin'
'bout, not anyways afore the colonel's wife
and a regiment of volunteers.

                           "Pray for me!" shouts Buller,
"pray for me for I is wrasslin' with the Enemy!"
Yer ding-dong right, thinks I. His hands is clutchin'
way around the place you cut the best steak outten
beef. The look of sufferin' on his face
begins to change. Now he's dancin' like
a real live Shaker. There's a look of panic comin'
over him. He's goin' over the edge, he's clutchin'
at his clawhammer coat. Zip, it comes right off.
Then it's his shirt, he's rippin' it off. Next
it's his suspenders, they go flyin'. Then
his pants, they go down, yessir, right down,
and he grabs aholt of them and bangs them down
against a bench, thinkin' somehow to get
them tenants out and on the road to someplace
else. But what comes out? It ain't the lizards.
It's shortbread biscuits. A double-bladed knife.
One chaw of tobacco. A corncob pipe. A flask
of antifogmatic corncob oil. Then, at the end,
three lizards—*whoosh!*

                      One of them goes flyin' off
and lit like a limp green horseshoe on the frontal development
of the colonel's lady. Well, not quite a lady—
she's big as a Belgian plowhorse. And nigh on as ugly.

60

There she sat, fannin' herself with a turkey
tail. That scamp of a lizard commenced to run
directly down the center of her breastbone. And kept
on runnin', I do believe. She was just bound
to faint and she done it all first-rate. She flung
the turkey tail straight up in the air. She give
one big histin' shake, then rolled on down
a slope and tangled up her legs and garters
in a huckleberry bush and jest lay still. By now
old Buller got nothin' on him but a pair of shoes
and woolen socks and eel-skin garters. He leaps
over the bench and lands both legs astraddle
our sergeant-major, shuttin' him up with a snap,
head atwixt his knees like he was shuttin' up
a jackknife.

By then you couldn't tell just who
was the sinner and who was the saved. All you could see
was Buller's pale white barley-butt recedin'
in a sea of uniforms. He weighed nigh on three hundred
pounds. He had this big black stripe like a bridle
rein a-runnin' down his back. They was cramp-knots
on his legs as big as walnuts and mottled splotches
on his shins. His belly was the size and color of a paunch
of beef. As he ran it was a-swingin' side to side.
He leaned back as he went and looked just like a feller
totin' a big bass drum. I couldn't help but shout

Them who smoke Havannies
All get a foul disease!
They get brainless as chimpanzees,
    They get meagre as lizards!
They go mad, they beat their wives!

They lead awful sinful lives!
They plunge carvin' knives
    Into their gizzards!

That was the end of Buller's preachin' days.
There ain't so many preachers run stark naked
past a colonel's wife and not do damage
to their character. You can bet your boots on that!

November 1846

The Conquest of Monterey

Yes, we pant to see our country and its rule
far-reaching. Decades of despots deprived the Mexicans
of an even chance of being happy and good.
Let us strike off their shackles. Let us make them free.

That said for the Mexicans, now we ask:
what has miserable, inefficient Mexico
to do with the goal that we are called to—to people
the New World continent with a noble race?

Monterey is ours. General Taylor made
short work of that. It is clinching proof
of the invincible energy of the Anglo-Saxon character.
Next we say: Let there be peace. Let
Mexico cede large areas to us. Let them
make way for a new mankind, for their everlasting good!

Walter Whitman, Editor
Brooklyn *Eagle*
November 1846

From a Letter to the
London Religious Observer

The question of our time is this: how to reform
mankind? In America, militant means are now
in vogue. But they rest on misconstruing man's capacities
and misrepresenting his place in the universe.

                                                    These
are not delusions out of medieval times. They are today's
intolerant methods of zealous prophets and reformers.
Through them, merciless irrational ambition has appropriated
for itself the language of brotherly love. Fanatical
belief in democracy has made democracy impossible.
Cloaked in a hocus-pocus of flattery, prophecy,
and deceit, "Manifest Destiny" holds sway. Mexico
is now its victim. What nation will be next?

December 1846

1847

♦ ♦

War: a byproduct of the arts of peace.

—AMBROSE BIERCE

♦ ♦

Perhaps all men, by the very act of being born, are destined to suffer violence; yet this is a truth to which circumstance shuts men's eyes. The strong are, as a matter of fact, never absolutely strong, nor are the weak absolutely weak, but neither is aware of this. They have in common a refusal to believe that both belong to the same species.

—SIMONE WEIL

♦ ♦

Harper's New Monthly Magazine

A Message to Our Readers

A New Year dawns; the nascent 1847 greets us. It is a time of reflection for all Americans.

In the past, we have regarded the separation of Church and State as essential to the American idea.

But a national Church is one thing and a national Religion is quite another. And in nothing are they more unlike than in their capacity to warm the spirits of a people and awaken a sense of Providence in their hearts.

We subscribe to belief in a national religion. It is made up, first, of the faith that our nation's institutions are divinely in-spired. Second, it asserts that they are inextricably bound up in the workings of Providence. Through the operation of the two there lies the real possibility of creating the Kingdom of God on earth.

Is our national Religion widely shared? Ask any American and you will soon learn that our American Constitution has a moral meaning and a sacredness over and above the fundamental laws of any other common-wealth. What is the reason for this?

First, we know in our hearts that the spirit of enterprise has made us a chosen people. Second, we know that the land which beckons us Westward is strikingly adapted to greatness—not just by its vastness, the spectacular features of its landscape or the plenitude of its harvests, but because it is particularly inspiriting of the greatness reserved to this nation and to this nation alone by our national Religion.

What is the nature of that greatness? It is the unparalleled opportunity for unleashing the intelligence, the sagacity, the energy, the restlessness, and the indomitable will of the Anglo-Saxon race.

Ours is the only race that masters physical nature without being mastered by it. Ours is the only race whose teeming millions have been hurrying Westward since the dawn of time.

Ours is the only race with a vital spirit which shelters the most intense home feelings, on the one hand, along with a love of enterprise and its venturesome sisters—the will to expand and the will to colonize.

Ours is the only race which fears nothing. It claims everything within its reach. It is the race which enjoys the future more than the present, and believes its destiny to be one of incomparable, immeasurable grandeur.

The Western Commonwealth of these United States is the land destined for that race—the promised land of a chosen people!

As it is written in the Book of Exodus 3:5,

> "Put off the shoes from thy
> feet, for the place where thou
> standest is holy ground!"

And as the poet writes,

> "Swift! To the head of the
> army!
> Swift! Spring to your places,
> Pioneers, O pioneers!"

January , 1847

A Note from an Adviser
to the President

We hear that Santa Anna has become the president
of Mexico once again. It is fitting such
a scoundrel be their El Supremo. However,
we lack an agent on the scene to test once more
his bottomless appetite for bribes. Civilian? Businessman?
Who?

      You have named Winfield Scott your general for the Vera
Cruz invasion. Scott and Taylor cannot
agree on splitting Taylor's troops to join
with Scott's. Sir, you must be the man and put
a stop to this. Order Taylor to give up his men.

I know I speak for others when I tell you most
respectfully that you must take upon yourself
these sorry details of the war. It is your undertaking.
General Scott is another military Whig.
Like Taylor, he has his Whig ambitions. But neither
holds the title of commander in chief. That
is for you and you alone. Let them push
and shove each other. You must play the statesman.
Like a father, you must set them straight. At times,
practical politics consists in ignoring facts.

January 1847

69

President Polk's Reply

Why, James, do you insist on writing
me at length of what I already
know?
      Bend your mind to the commissioning
of agents. Who would be up to the task
of corrupting the Great Corrupter?

                        The penny
press appears to be the second
hand on the clock of our success.
Why not Moses Beach of the New York *Sun*?

                            January 1847

Auras

Mister Andrew Jackson Davis, the "Seer of Poughkeepsie," author of The Philosophy of Spiritual Intercourse, Being an Explanation of Modern Mysteries; The Great Harmonia; etcetera; *on the subject of spiritualistic experiences relating to two personages known to him.*

Spiritual clairvoyance, mental illumination—these
are the marks of high enlightenment! The serene
interpenetration of certain intellects
must be the outcome of quickening intuitions.
It is the one, the only true, superior condition!

Joseph Wilbur, celebrated Trenton Quaker,
ran to his barn last week to saddle up
his horse, crying, "My neighbor Thomas Searl
is tying a rope in the loft of his barn to hang
himself! I see it clearly! I must go
before it is too late!" Off he sped
arriving just as the unhappy Searl was about
to jump from a beam with a noose around his neck.
Wilbur talked him out of most certain death.
An affectionate spirit! Spiritual clairvoyant!

♦ ♦

Then there is Mister E. A. Poe. He strives
to revive his magazine, the *Stylus,* and lectures here
upon his favorite topic, "The Universe." He is poor.
He lives in a state of tragic exaltation. He says
he would put all other thinkers in the land to shame.

Yet I am his star. He comes to me as a disciple.
His questions are wild and daring. What intellect!
What grasp of the Mystery! What forcing open of the prison
of the flesh to attain the world beyond! He has seen
visions of Thespesius and Xolena and the pale Astarte!

But one thing else I saw: his aura. His body
is enveloped in a shadow, one that goes before him
and hovers over him and follows him. An everlasting
shade. It has been his constant company since childhood.
The shadow of death. Yet he knows it not for what it is!

Poughkeepsie *Tribune*
January 1847

General Antonio Lopez de Santa Anna
Assumes the Title "President of Mexico"
for the Third Time

My México. A wondrous, magical expanse of land!
Nations of native peoples. Legions of languages.
Arrays of regions and climates. Each as it is,
each as it has been since the *conquista*.

                                    The government
is me. I tend my people. Do I impose
myself? Am I a dictator? Is President Polk
a dictator?
                Polk is no hero of a war with France,
I am. I have enjoyed power. But I have been an exile,
too, and I have come back. I have regained the power,
lost it, regained it once again.

                                It cost me
a leg in battle.

                    The Yankees have come out shopping
for half of Mexico. They are determined to have it
for their absolute dominion. They say that they
will tame it, enhance it, improve it—
                                they will do a very great deal
with it, you may be sure of that. They believe that they
alone possess the power to take this nation
for themselves. They think they enjoy this power
in perfect righteousness, by the grace of God.
The pale geometry of their greed will never overwhelm

my México. They have come to feel an appetite for conquest,
but in the end, She will eat them up! They will see, they will be
swallowed up—even General Taylor
knows this truth!

As for death, it is nothing personal
to die. If one expects nothing, one should hope for nothing.

We all go but one way, the way that leads
to where there are no flowers, no birds, no sounds.
As you go on, your steps get slower. The landscape all
around you turns dark and bare. The thought comes over you
that when you were born you were without hope, without fear. You
were simply born.

Now, in your return, you find
you are without fear once more. Without hope.
It is— there is— nothing. Nothing at all.

February 1847

Remarks Made by
Senator Thomas Hart Benton of Missouri
at the Springfield Lyceum

A few weeks ago Senator Benton returned to his home state of Missouri on a brief speaking tour. Ever a servant of the people and champion of the noblest of causes, he consented to speak to the Lyceum regarding our current war with Mexico. He favored the assembly with one of the most passionate and resounding pieces of oratory ever to spring from the lips of one known universally as an outstanding exponent of the art. Herewith, a summary of his remarks.

"Ladies and gentlemen. Most assuredly, our blessed nation
is moving west!

[*strong applause*]

But this is not an isolated movement.
It is only part, a fractional part of a movement
much more powerful, more inescapable than any
we have dreamed till now. The westward movement is nothing
more or less than a leading, a holy leading—
one the children of Adam have always felt—
to follow in the footsteps of the sun!

[*applause*]

Thousands are streaming
here from Europe. They join the columns wending
their way to the westernmost reaches of the continent.
From the beginning of time, westward has been the course
of heavenly bodies and westward the course of the human

race. And science and national power and civilization
inevitably have followed in their train!

[*strong applause*]

A few years hence
the Rocky Mountains will be behind us, the Pacific
shore achieved. Next the children of Adam
will set sail across the wide Pacific. Then
we shall complete the circuit of the globe! We
shall have Asia, ladies and gentlemen, we shall have that very
Asia where our divine forebears first were planted
by their Creator!

[*cheers*]

I, too, hail this event! I hail the footprints
of the Caucasian race upon the Pacific shore!
Think of the blessings of democracy spreading across
this continent! Think of that same democracy
moving across the sea to India, whose unhappy
millions are subject to British tyranny! And into
China, crushed by ancient despots! Think
of the effects it will have on commerce! Think what the spreading
of our faith will do to change their lives!

[*applause, with cries of "Hear! Hear!"*]

Yea,
the valley of the Columbia shall be the granary of China
and Japan! But first I tell you this—we must win
the war with Mexico! They have set their feet upon

our sacred soil! We must take them down, no matter
what the cost!

[strong applause with cries of "Hurrah!" for some minutes]

> When we win this war, we win
it all! Lose this war and we lose the destiny
which has been sealed to us! Missourians, patriots,
brave men all—accept the challenge, enlist
in the volunteer regiments! And to those who stay behind,
I say, "Give of your prayers, your gifts, and the fervor
of your souls! Let us write the history of this land in fiery
letters on the tablets of destiny! God bless America!"

*At this point, amidst the cheering multitude an impromptu parade was
formed. The senator was elevated to the shoulders of the stalwarts of
Springfield, and he was carried forth in a tumult of acclamation. It is need-
less to add that the senator's call for volunteers was met with the greatest
possible enthusiasm among the eligible Show-Mes, scores of whom clogged
the entrance of the recruiting office on the following morning.*

Springfield, Missouri, *Journal*
February 1847

The Battle of Buena Vista!

General Taylor's Triumph!
A Reprimand from the President!

Via our own dispatch boat
We are pleased to announce that a new correspondent now represents this newspaper and has joined General Taylor's army in northern Mexico. Mister S. L. C. is now engaged in other pursuits. We wish him well.

M. Beach, Publisher
The New York Sun

The *tug-of-war* between a Democratic president and a brilliant and beloved Whig general has now become more than just a phrase.

The plot: Mister Polk orders General Taylor to surrender 9,000 of his troops to General Scott for the attack by sea on Vera Cruz.

The result: the general understandably concludes that the true author of this decision is *Eris,* the goddess of discord and political intrigue. Congress has already authorized striking a gold medal in his likeness to commemorate his victory at Palo Alto. He is the favorite candidate of Whigs for president in 1848. What other reason could there be for the summary clipping of his wings?

True to his name, "Old Rough-and-Ready" disobeys the order and advances with 5,000 mostly untried volunteers against some 20,000 Mexican troops in a bloody battle at Buena Vista! Our losses, but 300! For the Mexicans, uncounted thousands! The war in northern Mexico is over! The army of Santa Anna is fled! Tales of gallantry are legion.

A few hours after the conclusion of the battle, a reprimand from

Secretary of War Marcy reaches General Taylor. For his brilliant but unauthorized triumph he is condemned to enforced idleness and summary chastisement!

[*From the reporter's notebook*]

General: "That slackjawed, sissy-pated son-of-a-bitching lawyer Polk couldn't order up his left great toe even if he had to. To this army he's proved to be a half-brother to cholera, he's as much a commander in chief as a bushel of rattlesnakes. He is a damned ambitious chicken-bred office clerk, and the wails of the dying must be music to his ears! Jumping Jesus, I'd rather roast in hell than eat breakfast with the man. You can bet your boots I'll kick him hell-west and crooked for saying I'm too inde-goddamnpendent!"

M. B., Jr.
February 1847

A Blessing

I abhor this war with Mexico. I would not appropriate
one square mile of Mexico by force.

I say,
"Let Nature's laws fulfil our destiny.
If we can extend our empire by the Christian arts
of peace and trade, it will be a blessing to the Mexicans,
to us, and to the world."

The Mississippi and the Amazon,
united! The United States, mother of a thousand
states, tropical and temperate, on either side
of the equator! One America, its population in the hundreds
of millions! The fulfillment of a mission—and our destiny!

Theodore Parker, abolitionist
March 1847

"Gentlemen, This Is No Humbug"

Imagine—the extraction of a tumor from your jaw without
torment! Imagine—the setting of a bone without
excruciation! Imagine—the banishment of pain
from medicine and dentistry! Doctor J. C. Warren's
newest compound, *sulfuric ether,* is shown
to be the worker of such miracles. A humble house painter,
Gilbert Abbot, bears witness to its powers. The eminent
Doctor Oliver Wendell Holmes has given it
his benediction, and names it "*anaesthetic.*"

◆ ◆

The newest in improved and fully graduated
magnetic machines! Fowler and Wells announce
the latest means for eradicating headaches,
deafness, palpitations, paralysis, *tic doloreux,*
acute and chronic headaches, bronchitis, rheumatism,
spinal affections, fits, general debility,
and dyspepsia. Professional consultations in our offices
at number 303 on Broadway, New York City.
Day and evening. Phrenology our specialty. Hydropathy
and dietetics. The laws that govern Life
and Health revealed! The spirit of Hope, Activity,
Self-Reliance, and Manliness made manifest!
Treatment, advice, and all progressive measures
that will Reform, Elevate, and Improve
Mankind.

Popular and scientific journals sold.

◆ ◆

For the use of young ladies in schools, for the elevation of their sex
by opening up to them a profession as educators
of the young, it is proposed that churchwomen in each of our cities
raise a hundred dollars for the dispatch of female
teachers to the Western Commonwealth. "Two million children
languish today without a teacher, while those
who go to school are relegated to the not-so-tender
mercies of hard unfeeling men too lazy
or too stupid to follow on the duties appropriate
to their sex." So says Mrs. Catharine Beecher,
who adds, "Instead of twining silk and conning
novels, let women become the best—as well
as cheapest—guardians of our children." Already hundreds
of teachers have assembled for instruction in Moral Training
at the hands of Mrs. Beecher. Soon they will find
their way West. We say to each and all, Godspeed!

American Woman's Magazine
March 1847

A Letter in Her Majesty's Diplomatic Pouch

To the Right Honourable Earl of Dunwoodie
c/o Ashburton and Williams, Solicitors
Gray's Inn
London

My Lord, and Gentlemen,

I am most honoured by your inquiries on behalf of Her Majesty's commission regarding our contribution to the advancement of scientific knowledge in these, Her former American colonies.

As I know you esteem forthrightness as a manly virtue as well as a scientific one, I will say that I began my work in the natural sciences out of a sense of outrage. Yes, I believe that is not too strong a term. Since childhood I had been taught that all of mankind derived from a single pair of ancestors, and that all diversities in the human species—all of what is now regarded as remarkable and worthy of study—were the result of the influences of climate, locality, food, etcetera.

As a youth, I asked myself: can it be true that man was created perfect and beautiful, and afterward, by the operation of chance and chance alone, underwent such changes as to present us today with an array of races ranging from the noblest Caucasian to the most degraded Australian and Hottentot?

I vigorously rejected entertaining such a view. If that was work of the Creator, then it betrayed an intellect similar to that of a careless and incorrigibly small-minded shopkeeper—the mind of one who could bring forth a magnificent species and then hand it over with indifference to the blind operations of chance!

I soon found myself communing with the remarkable, penetrating intelligence of Mister G. W. Pratt. Through his example and encouragement, I found myself possessed of another, nobler view of the matter, namely, that the various races of man came into being separately, and each of the races has had a distinct and fitting development according to its endowments.

In order to pursue further study of this notion, I was led to travel to the shores of the American continent where I have been quite free to pursue my investigations into the parallel development of the races. All of the races are represented here, although as yet examples of the yellow Asiatic race are somewhat lacking. Nevertheless, my study of the American savage Indian has led me to some tentative conclusions regarding the kinship of that group with the yellow Asiatics.

Let me add that in my years on American soil I have excited controversy as a result of my investigations. I found that if I could not agree to the commonplace idea of the Creator and His works, then I could not also, in good conscience , assent to one of the major political tenets of the American republic, that is, Mister Jefferson's *dictum* that by that same Creator, "all men are created equal," etcetera.

On the contrary, I concluded that the Creator in his wisdom fashioned the Negro as a separate and inferior race from ours. Whether or not the citizens of the southern states of this nation consider me their benefactor in holding that view is not entirely clear. They seem to prefer the familiar and consoling generalities of the Christian religion, which they attempt to bend in unnatural and illogical ways so as to preserve their admiration for Mister Jefferson, the teachings of the Christian faith, and the practice of chattel slavery, all at the same time. This seems to me to be a great knot of contradictions, and doomed to certain failure.

Mine is a simpler notion, and in science, as we know, the simpler explanation is always the one to be preferred.

The white and black races alike labour under a great weight of religious baggage on this issue. Furthermore, Americans are by temperament not given to the contemplation of complex questions; they desire that simple questions be asked, and simple answers be given. In recent weeks I have heard a distinguished American in public life opine on the current state of knowledge in the racial sciences, as follows: "The leopard may not change his spots, nor the Ethiopian his skin." *Ipse dixit.*

I regret that time does not permit a greater elaboration of my findings, or of my experiences here, as I am engaged to depart within the hour on an expedition to some large and interesting mounds to be found along the banks of the Ohio River.

It is said by the local inhabitants that these are relics of a city built by a prehistoric American Indian tribe. I think it is quite unlikely that this is true, but in the interests of science, one is obliged to make inquiries.

With my apologies for the unavoidable haste in which this letter must be written, I subscribe myself as your most faithful servant, and student of science and the study of humanity,

Samuel Chilton, M.A.
March 1847

Dispatch to General Winfield Scott

General Scott: To be delivered directly into your hands by Mr. B. Traven, confidential courier. For your eyes only.

Consulate of the United States of America
Mexico City
March 12, 1847

My Dear General Scott:

This letter is to call to your attention an encounter which you must sustain shortly with a most singular personage. Allow me to write you these few words by way of explanation.

♦ ♦

Apparently the president has become very susceptible to the opinions of the editors of the New York penny press. The meanest and most successful of these enterprises, the *Sun,* is published by Mister Moses Beach, who leads a faction advocating taking all of the territory of Mexico by force. He predicts that our next president will be the "prominent man of either party who comes out for the occupation of all of Mexico, the purchase of Cuba, and replacement of our present rotten and useless navy."

In his work, Beach is aided by a woman journalist named Mrs. Jane McManus Storms. A Catholic and a person fluent in Spanish, she is known extensively to the inner circles of the New York Catholic clergy. The president's inner circle is unanimous in regarding these people as "wonderful," as "real hopers," and as "persons who intimately appreciate the importance of the doctrine of Manifest Destiny to our nation."

Beach and Storms are convinced that the Catholic church in Mexico wishes the war to end soon. Such a quick end to the war would also coincide perfectly with the president's desires. Beach maintains that there are rational principles upon which the war might end: viz., "to occupy and annex all of Mexico and secure a direct route to the Pacific Ocean *for the good of the world.*" I am sure that you, with your small force that has but recently landed at Vera Cruz, will appreciate the obvious consequences of such a notion.

In return for his services it is understood that the president has promised him as a broker's fee a permanent right-of-way from the Atlantic to the Pacific Ocean for a means of transit across the Isthmus of Tehuantepec, as well as a banking concession in Mexico City and such additional concessions as may be negotiated.

Some weeks ago the two landed at Tampico, whence they made their way to Mexico City. To the world, he was said to be on a "business trip." He was carrying introductions to church leaders, and Storms was accompanying him as his interpreter. They arrived in Mexico City early in January of this year but their success was confounded by the very press they represent. The New Orleans *Picayune* found out about their mission and reported on their progress in some detail. And while on board ship in transit to Tampico, Mister Beach encountered a former Mexican diplomat whom he had known as publisher of the *Sun* in New York City.

The result has been distrust and resistance of the two at every step, even by the leaders of the Mexican church. At the time of their arrival, Santa Anna was not in Mexico City. He had gone to the north to oversee the fighting against General Taylor's forces. In Santa

Anna's absence, Beach immediately urged the clerics in Mexico City to resort to armed rebellion in order to shorten the war and win benefits for themselves. On the spur of the moment he also supplied $40,000. of his own personal funds to pay the salaries of any pro-church troops who would so oblige.

You may imagine the anomaly of my position: as of two weeks ago, Santa Anna was preparing to fight General Taylor's forces in the north; you had landed at Vera Cruz with your forces and were preparing to undertake the siege of that city; and a New York newspaper publisher was in Mexico City, financing a civil war at the rear of both forces without my knowledge.

When the news of your siege of Vera Cruz reached Santa Anna he promptly returned to Mexico City. He thereupon invited Beach to an audience in the National Palace, which the man actually intended to accept until I told him he would certainly be taken under arrest and that he should flee immediately to Tampico and escape by packet boat.

Before leaving, however, Beach asked *la* Storms to find a way to penetrate the enemy lines by coach and interview you personally about these events. She continues to write letters to the *Sun* advocating that we act with "firmness and liberality" to take large portions of Mexico into the Union in order to assure a "full right of way for the United States to build a railroad or a canal across the Isthmus of Tehuantepec."

She will arrive, perhaps simultaneously with this letter. As consul of the United States still accredited to a nation with which we are officially at war, I find it advisable to maintain the greatest discretion in all of my official relations with every unit of government, with my own as much as that of Mexico.

I trust, therefore, that you will make immediate and appropriate use of this information.

Yours most sincerely,

John Black, Consul of the United States

General Scott's Reply to Consul Black

Consul Black: To be delivered directly into your hands by Mr. B. Traven, confidential courier. For your eyes only.

U.S. Army—temporary Headquarters
Vera Cruz, Mexico
March 29, 1847

My dear Sir,

I am most grateful to you for yours of the 12th inst. It so happened that it arrived on the 19th. Mrs. Storms appeared at my tent on the 20th, only a few days before I was to commence the bombardment of the city of Vera Cruz, and with a story not unlike the one you have recounted to me.

She is very much a "pusher." I listened for some minutes to her notions of "a greater power, even, than Manifest Destiny, which has assumed control of the fortunes of the people of Mexico, and do what they will, pulls them inexorably toward complete integration into the Republic of the Stars and Stripes," etcetera, etcetera.

I found her outrageously smooth. She writes, it seems, under the male pseudonym "Montgomery."

I heard her out and sent her on her way.

She and Beach have been meddling in something about which they have exactly the wrong notions. Do they imagine I can win and then occupy a country roughly the size of our own with a mere 20,000 troops, only a few of whom know how a war is conducted, much less an occupation?

You may let it be known both to Secretary of State Buchanan and the president that they are to send no more worthless messages to this command by way of a plenipotentiary in petticoats.

Yours truly,

W. Scott, General
U.S. Army

Vera Cruz—Besieged and Taken!

From the Picayune's *own special correspondent with General Scott's forces—A special service by packet boat directly to our offices in New Orleans—The Very First Report!*

Shells bursting in air by day! Great arcs of fire
in the night sky! A fortress impregnable four hundred years
and a city hid in walls made eight feet thick!
Our invading force—twelve thousand men,
the greatest force to come by sea since the time
of Greece's Alexander!
                 The genius of General Scott!
A strategy so bold, so novel, the Mexicans had no
notion what befell them. The usual amenity,
a call for surrender, was summarily rejected. The general
then began to pour the greatest concentration
of artillery fire known in modern times
from both his land emplacements and his ships, day
after day and night after night into both fort and city
catching the Mexicans completely by surprise.
                         The fire
of the Mexicans went wild. Fell short. Fell silent. Meanwhile
the siege went on. Flames and smoke, explosions,
wails and screams from behind the city walls.
At length, the flag of surrender. Vera Cruz was ours!
We understand the havoc wrought was frightful. A shell
fell on a hospital during surgery. The light
restored, the patient was found—torn to pieces!
Pleas for letting foreigners, women, and children
flee were dismissed by General Scott. "I warned them

to expect the worst," he said. Only when Mexican
General Landero begged for terms the shelling ceased.
Modern weaponry has saved the lives of hundreds
of our troops! In just two days the siege was ended!
Mexican casualties in the hundreds. Our losses, sixty-seven.
Mexican troops surviving were paroled, stacked their arms,
and marched out through the city gate to the tune
of "Yankee Doodle." A triumph for General Scott!

S. L. C.
April 1847

The Triumph of the Anglo-Saxon Race
and Manifest Destiny

Part I

The Susquehanna Philological Society of Philadelphia, Pennsylvania, herewith publishes in its Acta *the first of three installments of a spirited colloquy held in its rooms during April 1847 between the following noted medical and scientific personages:*

PROF. CHARLES WHITE, M.D, surgeon and exponent of the new science of ethnology, of London, England, now residing in New York City;

MR. PHINEAS CHEVEUX, M.A., of Tilliesburg, South Carolina, scientist and founder of the American Trichological Society; and

MR. ORSON FOWLER, P.P., of Boston, widely known as the "Oracle of Practical Phrenology," who, with his brother Lorenzo is currently conducting an extended series of lectures and demonstrations in this city.

♦ ♦

DR. CHARLES WHITE: With deference to the generosity and good intentions of the patrons of this newly formed society, I must say at the outset that I am the only person here who is qualified to hold an opinion on the topic. The question of the races touches upon the nascent science of ethnology. My years of close observation in the practice of medicine have qualified me to stand today before you as the chief spokesman for that science—

MR. ORSON FOWLER: Sir, I beg to differ.

MR. PHINEAS CHEVEUX: And I too! I differ wholly and completely with what you have just said.

WHITE: I merely said that I—

FOWLER: You distinctly said, "My years of close observation in the practice of medicine."

WHITE: Yes, I did. That is exactly what I said. In the practice of medicine—

FOWLER: Practice! Is all you doctors can speak of "practice"? What could possibly be the truth of any observation coming from a so-called science if it is undertaken for "practice"? There is a finer motive which others possess in their scientific endeavors. We phrenologists share a deep desire to uplift mankind—

CHEVEUX: And I say that doctors of medicine are nothing more than purveyors of pretentious humbug. Not knowing the exact cause of an illness, you jolly your patients without mercy so that they will think you are wise. Tell us, Doctor White, what precisely is your theory of medicine? Or does your practice of medicine even have a theory?

WHITE: What are you two about? First you slander my profession. Then you introduce arbitrary notions about "uplifting mankind" and a "theory" of medicine—

CHEVEUX: Sir, if I seem offensive it is only in the interests of truth and exact observation. I am the founder of a science, the science of trichology. I examine the data of the natural world scrupulously, ruthlessly. Then I proceed to clear the air, casting out the dross of superstition. I reveal all, without fear or favor. I follow in the steps of Socrates!

WHITE: That is ludicrous, sir. Socrates didn't know a fig about science or medicine or this trichology you say that you—

FOWLER: And I repeat that of the three of us, I am the only one who has always acted out of the deep desire to promote the welfare of humankind.

CHEVEUX: You, sir? And what about me? What of my desires? As if I weren't in it for a noble reason.

WHITE: "It"? What "it" are you in, pray?

CHEVEUX: Science. The faithful description of nature.

FOWLER: And what of mercy? And intellectual enlightenment? What of the future of the human species?

CHEVEUX: That future is already quite clear.

FOWLER: Pardon me, I did not know I stood in the presence of a seer. You have godlike knowledge of the future, sir?

CHEVEUX: Yes, the future is quite clear to me.

WHITE: Mister Cheveux, you must let us in on this cosmic cognition of yours. What is the future of the human species? I cannot wait to hear.

CHEVEUX: Quite simply, it can be read in the study of a single human hair. It is all there, written quite as clearly as in a book.

WHITE: Such a view, sir, is beyond the competence of reasoned discourse.

CHEVEUX: Do not scoff, sir, reflect. Good investigation is a matter of paying scrupulous attention to the facts. From observation of facts and facts alone the inquiring mind may begin to apprehend their relationships, and then go on to formulate theories about them. Fact: human beings have hair. Fact: hair survives through centuries of time. Fact: hair samples of the different races from different millennia may be studied and compared with one another. No, do not interrupt, hear me: I am the curator of the world's largest collection of hair. The Secretary of the Interior has sent out circulars to his Indian agents to collect hair in my name. From every corner of the globe missionaries forward hair to me, hair taken from the very heads of those whose souls they have saved. Egyptologists have sent me mummy hair. I have hair from the head of Napoléon Bonaparte and George Washington, Andrew Jackson, and Bartola the female Aztec dwarf, and Bigwater the Indian chief—

FOWLER: Spare us the ludicrous particulars.

CHEVEUX: I have pursued hair on every continent and from every century. I am the world's foremost trichologist. I am the very personification of the science of hair. I have pursued trichological knowledge, and now after decades of patient work, I have written *Omnia Trichia: The History and Hierarchy of Human Hair.*

WHITE: Oh, Cheveux, this is absurd.

CHEVEUX: Absurd? It is my magnum opus!

FOWLER: You pretend to spread the blessings of intellectual enlightenment by being the author of a tome on the subject of hair? Nonsense. Now, I am a practitioner of a truly edifying scientific discipline. From my home office in New York I publish books and tracts, I run a museum, I sell equipment to my fellows in practice, and of course I continue to perfect my skills in the most signal and sensitive vocation of all.

CHEVEUX: Which is?

FOWLER: Why, the phrenological arts.

WHITE: You mean you read head bumps? Why not read palms, or divine sheep entrails, or meditate on the flight of birds?

FOWLER: Because I get results, and for a scientist nothing succeeds like success. So great is my success that my brother and I have expanded our investigations into new and related fields.

WHITE: Really? Such as?

FOWLER: Such as mesmerism. What mysteries of mind and body may be unlocked in the mesmerical state! And then, there is hydrotherapy. It is the ultimate ablution, the cure for both body and soul. In addition, I give counsel on hygiene and marriage—

WHITE: Good Lord! That?

FOWLER: A delicate subject, I agree, but it is of the greatest importance. Especially to the members of our female society.

CHEVEUX: You can't—you—surely you don't talk about "it"!

FOWLER: Of course I do. And finally, and most apropos, I have taken up the cause which will be the salvation of our republic, the cause which will preserve the American home and the family, teetotal temperance. There now, gentlemen, I have said. What say you?

WHITE: I say that a spurious question about theory was raised in a typically offhand and inattentive manner by Mister Cheveux some minutes ago. Now I propose a truly scientific question for us to consider. It is the scientific question of principle. For example, if there is gradation of any kind in nature, then nature will employ it not just in one instance only, but as a general principle. My work in the measurement of hundreds of human skulls has made it quite clear that there are gradations of mankind as reflected in the sizes and shapes of those skulls. And by continued observation it has become clear to me that these gradations are not merely confined to the dimensions of the skull, but to many other parts of the human anatomy as well. For example, the penis of the African male is larger than that of the European—

FOWLER: What? What are you saying?

WHITE: It has been shown in every anatomical school in London. It is a fact. Mister Cheveux, you will back me up. You have said that facts are important, have you not, sir?

CHEVEUX: The penis of the African male in South Carolina is—

FOWLER: The penis is a subject which is not to be discussed in a public forum!

WHITE: The penis is an observable fact, sir. And this is not a public forum. It is a colloquy conducted by a philological society, which is something quite different. Now, may I proceed? It is also clear that the various species, that is to say (and better called) the races of mankind were originally created separately, and distinguished by marks of various kinds. Skin color, for example: we know the races as brown, yellow, black, and white, for those colors mark them infallibly. Now, as with all animals, the races do interbreed, but this fact comes to nothing because we have observed another principle at work in human reproduction: the species criterion of infertility in animal interbreeding.

CHEVEUX: Infertility, you say? As between whites and blacks, I haven't noticed any signs of infertility. In my hometown in South Carolina—

WHITE: I am speaking here of a principle, the species criterion of infertility in animal interbreeding. If you breed different species of dogs—foxes with wolves, or hyenas with jackals—such inter-breeding produces sterile offspring.

CHEVEUX: Mules, you mean?

WHITE: I am speaking at the moment of dogs, but now that you have brought up mules, yes.

CHEVEUX: Mules and dogs are one thing, but my experience in South Carolina is that the human races behave differently.

WHITE: I am speaking here of a principle, the application of the species criterion of infertility in interbreeding.

FOWLER: I fail to understand what possible significance this dog-and-mule principle of yours is supposed to have for us human beings.

WHITE: It is a principle! It is a principle! Every principle is of the highest importance, don't you understand? Tell me, how, in principle, did the distinctions between the races arise? If the Negro, the savage American Indian, and some of the Asiatic tribes all arose from some common ancestor, then they could have changed into their present-day forms only as a result of climate and habitat. But if we say that, then we run the risk of saying that the entire animal kingdom was originally derived from one single ancestral pair!

Here ends the first installment. Two further installments will be published in succeeding numbers of the Acta.

April 1847

The Newest Thing in Hotels

we hear, is Boston's
Tremont House. Unparalleled in comfort and amenity
it rises day by day above its small-bore
neighbors. Its lobby boasts a dozen banks

of crystal chandeliers. Already added
is a wing called "Texas," and in process of completion is a wing
called "Oregon."

And when shall we see "Old Mexico, the Annex"?

Saint Louis *Reveille*
April 1847

Mister Polk Takes a Buggy Ride

"I cannot believe it, sir!" the president declares. Judge Mason shrugs. The buggy bumps and dips in the mudholes on Fourteenth Street. Silence. Then he goes on: "Calhoun is wholly destitute of principle. Supporting Taylor? That Whig, alias Federalist? Then all Calhoun's professions of states' rights must needs be false! Three years ago the man was set to nullify and dissolve the Union over tariffs. Now the tariffs have been reduced. It is my administration that has done the work. But he mounts a political hobby every month—first the tariffs, then the slavery question, now Taylor as candidate for president. I'm glad I dropped him from the Cabinet!"

The buggy turns up N Street. The evening air is heavy. Judge Mason knows his role. The president will vent, and he will listen.

Is there no one in the White House who would do the same? No need to answer. The Calhoun tittle-tattle isn't true, but the feelings are.

The president falls silent, then starts in again. "Two weeks ago the Cabinet agreed on terms to offer to the Mexicans to end the war. Dispatches in from Santa Fe announce our triumph there. Chihuahua City, also. But the New York *Herald* writes with great particularity about the embarkation of Mister Trist as my personal representative on a mission to Mexico. A profound cabinet secret! There has been treachery somewhere! The *Herald* gives aid and comfort to the enemy! The Mexicans hope their friends will come to power here in our next election. They will start to drag their feet, and then . . ."

"And then?" Judge Mason asks. The subject changes. "California! Nothing but collisions. General Kearny and Commodore Stockton argue over who is to hold the power there. And Lieutenant Colonel Frémont has sided not with Kearny but with Stockton, and for this he is in the wrong. Must I bring him back to Washington and try him in court-martial? If I do I'll have to deal with his father-in-law, Senator Benton—the doughty knight of the stuffed cravat! When the Senator holds forth he showers the Senate with his own particular philosophy three days at a go. Imagine his son-in-law brought home in chains!"

A pause. "General Tom Thumb," the president says. "Have you seen him? Truly a remarkable person. We had him in the parlor yesterday. I asked the Cabinet to walk down with me and see him. We found a number of ladies and gentlemen already there, and he was holding forth. Imagine a person so diminutive exhibited at all the principal courts of Europe." Another pause. "Celebrity. So easily attained—"

"So needful to a man in public life," the judge breaks in. "Frémont is the perfect case."

"You speak my mind. It's true—it's all too true," the president rejoins. "Celebrity so easily attained so soon will serve to grease a fall from greatness."

April 1847

At War with Mexico

From The Notebook of Colonel Bryant Blessing of the Massachusetts
Volunteer Cavalry

Leaving Vera Cruz we rode in columns
toward a line of foothills. Two snowcapped mountains
framed the far horizon, invitations to an upland
where hot humid winds and sand and sun will soon
be only memories.

♦ ♦

                    In a while we could look back and down
at the coast we left behind. Our fleet at anchor
in the harbor. City and fort a smoking mass
of ruins. Wagon trains and infantry
a long blue tail behind us. And along the shore,
as far as the eye could see, white lines of tents.
From on high they look like handkerchiefs the Lord
has seemed to strew in perfect symmetry,
a sign that we have come and we will stay.
Nothing will ever be the same for Mexico.

♦ ♦

But the tents. To be there is to see the fever and the jaundice,
smell the excrement and *vomito,* sense the deep
despair of surgeons treating such diseases
as are unknown in Boston and Poughkeepsie.
We leave behind not just a regiment, but a quarter
of our force.

                    We cannot arrive in a more temperate place
too soon.

How to face an army numbered in the scores
of thousands with a force so fallen, I do not know . . .

◆ ◆

Offhand, out of nowhere. More by insinuation
than insistence. Worming its way through the acrid smell
of saltpeter and the piss-sharp smells of cavalry. Dancing
across the gloss of sweat of men and horses
a slender shaft of odor, so clean and clear—

mesquite. The smell of its smoke rising in thin
invisible fingers from fires you will never see,
lost in a labyrinth of green ravines,
arroyos, gaps, and gullies tumbling beneath us
as we wend higher, ever higher on the road
to Puebla.

I think: *Old Mexico! This is its smell.*
What Cortez caught wind of when he left the Mosquito Coast
for the snowcapped Sierra Madres!
We move on. The thought has made me mettlesome. This
is the road of the conquerors. This is the road that leads
to the palaces that Prescott calls

The halls of the Montezumas!

April 1847

The Father of His Country

How many of us have remarked upon the hut on the east lawn of the Capitol? Within, and artfully hidden from the public's gaze, is Mister Horatio Greenough's sculpture of George Washington. Duly commissioned, heroically proportioned, done in Italy in bluish marble, the Father of Our Country is seated, naked to the waist, delivering up a sword.

We ask, "What will, or can, be done with Mister Greenough's work?" Too small for a pyramid, too grand for a graveyard, clutching a sword with a blade no bigger than a potato masher, the general seems to beg, "Take my sword if you will, but bring me my shirt!"

May it mercifully remain concealed until the next millennium. Then may it come forth and find new life, and be rechristened "The Spirit of the Artist, the Alien, and the Effete."

National Intelligencer
Washington, D.C.
April 1847

James Beckwourth at Santa Fe
and the Taos Pueblos

So I done my little service down to Santy
Fe, an' arter, me an' a partner set up
the best saloon fer faro, fandango dancin',
an' agwardenty you ever seen. It all went
fit to split 'til the day we heerd
the guvner had gone under out at Touse. An' not
jest him, them Purblos kilt a passel of Americans!
Wall, you see them injuns war mighty mad
fer the 'Mericans to come right in thar diggins, takin'
ever'thin' so easy-like. Thar kind of blood
is bad an' sneakin', an' they swore to count thar coups
in secret. So when Charlie (the guvner, Charlie Bent—
he was my frien' an' tradin' partner), went
out to Touse to see his wife (he got
a local wife—a real Doña an' a beauty),
they charged his house 'fore sunrise. The portal war too strong.
So they hacked it down with axes an' a Purblo cached
behint a pile of 'dobies shot him with a Nor'west
fusee, twice.

        Right then they done the same to both
him an' Liel, the district attorney. They drug 'em
through the streets, naket, skulpt alive,
eyes punched out, a-prickin' 'em with lances. No matter
how they begged 'em would they kill 'em, they
jest laughed. Then Stephen Lee, the brother of the gen'ral,
was kilt an' skulpt on his own housetop. Narcisse

Beaubien, son of the presidin' judge, was skulpt
an' killed. An' Anton, his slave, they done him the same.

"Kill the young'uns! Nits grows into lice"—
that war what they cried. But when they kilt
Narcisse, they kilt one of their own. He'd been away
to college in M'ssouri. That war his only crime.

So me an' Gen'ral Price an' a comp'ny of troops,
we hit the trail to Touse. Hawgs an' dawgs
war workin' over the remains. I reco'nized ol' Charlie,
what was left of 'im, an' twenty more besides.
Them Purblos now war all holt up in Touse
church, with its 'doby walls an' not a winder
facin' outen it. We tried bombardin', but that
funked out.

                 So then I tuck a axe an' cut
a breach what went half-way through a six-foot wall.
I war puttin' a cannon up to 'er to far a shell
on through, when one of our greenhorn gunners shot
a mortar shell. Wall, it fell short, right
at my boots! I pickt that sucker up an' shoved 'er
inter the breach I'd cut. Then did we
hightail it!
                 One blast did it all! We run
our cannon up an' poured in fire. Some boys
stormed the door. Some others fired the roof.
Thar war shoutin', thar war shells a-burstin', thar war wounded
screamin'. A Purblo comes a-runnin' toward me
yellin' "Bueno! Bueno! Me like Americanos!"
Says I, "You like Americanos? Take this sword

an' kill some Purblos. Ya!" He tuck the sword
an' run away. I gets this feelin' kinder
like a cow with a G'lena pill in her lights. Whar's
he goin' with my M'ssouri toothpick? Who's he killin'?
In a flick he's back and says, "Muchos muertos!"
Thar's blood on the blade. Of a sudden, I feel it's me
what's on the warpath.

        "Then you oughter die
fer killin' yer own people." That's what I says,
an' I'm not thinkin' anymore.

        I shot 'im dead.

End of April thar war a trial. Señora Bent
p'inted out the Purblo what had kilt her Charlie. He sot thar,
still, eyes squar' on her. He didn't show
a thing, not one tic, all the way
to the gallers.
        Señora Bent, she'd come to court,
Kit Carson's wife along. Now thar's a woman
to break yer heart! One peep of 'er eye an' yer life
will go direckly up in smoke! Woo-haugh!
This yere's the life fer me—Touse an' Santy Fe!

                April 1847

The Life and Adventures of Miss Eliza Allen, Volunteer

Being the truthful and well-authenticated narrative of a young lady of Eastport, Maine; her determination to follow one of whom her parents disapproved; her flight in man's attire; her enlistment; and her participation in the terrible battle of CERRO GORDO in the company of the troops of General Scott

The beginning of it all was innocent and unalloyed.
Bill Billings and Eliza Allen—she
loved him, and he loved her. He, a day laborer's
son. She, the minister's daughter. For the rings
and locks of hair and all the whispered promises
of love, their fathers and their mothers deigned them nothing
but anger and contempt.

◆ ◆

Why is it ever thus,
that parents never seem to comprehend
"It is not with her who walketh to direct her steps
but with an overwhelming power that controls her actions
and her ends"?

◆ ◆

No. "She has stooped too low." "He is out of his
     class."
They must never see or speak or write each other
on pain of her disinheritance.

◆ ◆

She is impaled.
To obey will make her wretched and destroy the life

of one she deeply loves. Refuse, and she
will be condemned to everlasting exile.

♦ ♦

                              Then a stroke
straight out of ancient myth. Rather than remain
and play Job's comforter, Bill enlists in a company
of volunteers and sails for Mexico.
With that, the cards Eliza holds have suddenly
changed their faces. The lives of Deborah Sampson
and Lucy Brewer come to mind. The first
had served as soldier in the army of the revolution. The second
sailed as top-man on the frigate *Constitution*
in the recent war with England. Each one had served,
each one had been discharged with honor. And so
a reverie becomes a thought, the thought a preoccupation,
preoccupation a fixed idea—she will go to Mexico,
she will join him! She will share in his life—share everything—
and through her love for him will do such deeds
as win respect, celebrity, and honor.

♦ ♦

A bundle of men's clothing, hidden in the barn. An hour
spent with a pair of scissors in a nearby grove.
She emerges shorn and newly dressed. No longer
is her name Eliza Allen. She is a young man of Eastport,
Maine, life savings in his pocket.

♦ ♦

                              At the docks, she boards
a ship for Portland. She overhears the mate. He asks
the captain who the young man is who has come
on board? The captain doesn't know or care,
he's had a good fat passage out of him. Suddenly
Eliza sees she has forgot the obvious. What
is her name? It is the first of many lessons she must learn.

At every step, nothing may be left to chance.
"George Mead" is the name she chooses.

♦ ♦

                              The lines are cast off,
they put to sea, and the ocean's pitch and roll
soon makes her ill. It is said that nothing makes
a man or woman seem more saintly than seasickness.
Not so, aboard this schooner. She must vomit at the rail
and be the butt of every sailor's joke.
They call her Pukeface Georgie.

♦ ♦

                              Portland. She goes
to a barber, an old black man who will trim her hair
to a male appearance. "'Markable hair," he says,
"fine as a lady's!" unconscious of the truth. One more
reminder—nothing can be left to chance!

♦ ♦

                              Now
to be recruited. She asks the barber where the office
is. "Orfis*uh,* not orfice," he laughs. "Ya'll see
a 'cruitin' sergeant struttin' round as pop'lar
as a hen wif one chickling, an' two li'l fellers a-drummin'
an' a-fifin' arter him. He got twenty rooster tails
stuck onter his hat an' eenamost brass a-bobbin'
on his shoulders an' figureed onter his coat an' trousis
as to make a six-pound brass cannon on!"

♦ ♦

                              Eliza
watches others volunteer. She sees that she
must be examined by a doctor. Unless she finds
a way around it, all is lost. A new
recruit comes up and tells her, "Don't you want
to go to Mexico? My company is short by one.

We've got the best set of officers and men in all
these diggin's. Sign up! We'll give them Mexicans hell!"
Eliza tells him of an injury she's had. "We got
a man worse off than you! If'n I don't get
you in, I'll give you my ears—and don't you dare
misdoubt it!" Off they go to a tavern full
of officers. When asked, one officer replies, "Yer
willin'? Yer able? Yer clear of disease? Ye kin do
yer duty like a sojer?" To this, Eliza
nods her head. "Go grab yer gear. Yer in."

♦ ♦

Another ship. Two weeks at sea, Portland
to Vera Cruz. Eliza's stomach learns
to heave and roll in concert with the swells.
Her face is tawny. Her voice is low and coarsened.
Her hands are bronzed and blistered, and her hair in knots.

No longer is she Private Mead. She is Eastport Georgie.

♦ ♦

Vera Cruz. The siege just ended. The aftermath
of shelling. Ruins everywhere. Palls
of acrid smoke. The stench of corpses. Houses,
churches, schools reduced to rubble. And even
yet, the drawn-out, agonizing groans of Mexicans
still buried under masses of timber and brick.
Where a shell has dug a crater, bloody stains
fan out. A foot, a leg, an arm lie begging
to be reclaimed. Now a body turns
its darkening face toward her, struggling and gasping
in its death throes like a single fish thrown up on shore
by a cruel and careless angler. The farther she walks
the more she sees: crushed heads and shattered limbs,
bodies with brains and hearts and lungs exposed,

eyes blown out of their sockets. And one or two,
still alive and shivering, begging for a bit
of bread or a sip of water.

It strikes at her deepest
fears. What of her lover? She can now see fates
for him far worse than any she had dreamed.

♦ ♦

Now
like a torpid serpent, the army starts its long
march into the mountains. The *vomito* has cut their numbers.
Nine thousand men. It's a puny excuse
for an invasion force. But for Eliza, be
they nine or ninety thousand, it is all the same—
how to find her lover in that mass of men?

♦ ♦

She asks, she looks, to no avail. Maine
volunteers are there, but where? The army moves
relentlessly. The landscape turns to mountains, streams,
forests. Nights are cold. Rumor follows
hard on rumor.

Santa Anna's army
lies in wait at a hill called Cerro Gordo.

♦ ♦

At last, she sees the enemy. But now it is through
new eyes. The Mexicans are in panoply. Their lancers'
steel-tipped spears reflect the sun like mirrors.
Their shells rain down from fortified emplacements. Rank
upon rank of infantry is dressed in black shakos, white cartridge
belts, their uniforms bright red and green. It is a stunning
image of an army. It makes the road-worn Yankee
troops look pitiful.

◆ ◆

Bugle calls are lost
in the roar of cannon and crackling musket fire.
Colors blur in the smoke and mist. And then
a brutal hand-to-hand with knives and swords
and bayonets, the yelling and the screams—and then the cries
of victory!

◆ ◆

Slashed in the arm by a cavalryman's sword,
Eliza falls. She hears the drums and bugles, sees
a bloody Stars and Stripes rising above
the smoke and mist. The firing wanes. Then nothing.

Only the chorus of the dying can be heard.
It seems an animal with a thousand voices, each crying
out for help.
And what, oh what, of her lover?

◆ ◆

She is carried to a surgeon. She fears not only for her life,
she fears for her discovery. Loss of blood
has made her weak. Dreamy. How can she bring
herself back?

Then the sound of a voice. "How
is his wound? Is it dangerous?" She has not heard that voice
for months, but she knows. It cuts right through to her soul
and brings her to her feet. The surgeon comes and brings
a cordial, and from the haze of her half-consciousness Eliza
sees the image of her lover loom large as life.
He too is wounded, he too is swathed in bandages,
yet he cares for a comrade more than himself—not knowing
who it is.

♦ ♦

Slowly, gently, she lets her voice
return to the tones that he will recognize. She summons
up the images of Eastport and their carefree days.

"Eliza, can it be you?" he cries. She takes his hand.
"It is," she whispers. "And I am yours forever."

♦ ♦

That was what the surgeon witnessed, and their tale
was wonderful to hear. It spread among the troops
like prairie fire. Lovers and heroes both,
the two had measured up to the most merciless of tests.

♦ ♦

The story of Eliza's trials precede them as they make
their way to Eastport.

The parents welcome them.
They see Eliza's love for Bill is pure.
But also sinewed strong, like steel.

They give consent.

♦ ♦

So she is remembered—Eliza Allen,
a girl of perfect courage, who did unwitnessed
what others only hope to brag of, someday,
somewhere, with the whole world looking on.

April 1847

Reading with the Fingers

Doctor Howe has brought a group of pupils
down from Boston. One in special, Laura
Bridgman, mute and blind and dumb from scarlet
fever, astonished all by reading from a Bible
done in *letters raised upon the page.*
How could we tell? By means of signs by hands
and fingers, she communicates the text.

What wonders

can be done with patience and ingenuity!
How does one do the same in dealing with his generals?

James K. Polk, *Diary*
May 1847

The Sacred Image

From our special correspondent currently travelling in the United States

The Daguerrian gallery is much in vogue. "Sun portraits,"
they are called. Some are of distinguished persons,
some of the commonest of the common, all exactly
as they come from the *camera obscura.* Their faces stare
from gallery walls, floor to ceiling, room
after room. No city is without the trade.

Memorials of affection, testaments of a thousand human
histories, the rows of faces briefly slake
what seems to be a quenchless American thirst
for history made personal. How else to explain the throngs
who come to view the visages of those who can be
nothing to them?

                What can one possibly see
in fifty score of faces? Simple homilies
of the nation's destiny? Intimations of a great experience
that may be shared by all who come to view
and pay the penny?

                Behold the portrait eyes!
They seem to say, "We share in the life, and have done,
since Jamestown and Plymouth Rock. Behold, our numbers
swell, and we shall have dominion over

every rock and field and mountain. *That has been our destiny—and it is manifestly yours!"*

C. D.

The Times of London

July 1847

Dissent in the Senate

*The senator from Ohio having yielded his time, the senator from Illinois
made the following remarks.*

If anything were wanting to prove that this is truly
an age of imbecility and truthless philosophy,
today it is made manifest in all the drivel
about the races. The "Anglo-Saxon race"
and the "Celtic race" and this race and that are passed off
as the latest word of science. They account for all
of history. And most of all, for the curse of slavery!

What is this "racial" theory? Consider, gentlemen:
the British long have wished to eradicate the Irish
population. They find our people odious,
ungovernable. We are the "Celtic race."
They wish to substitute their own, their "Anglo-
Saxon" people in our place. And they are doing
a damned good job of it—they are starving out the Irish,
and for all the world to see! And now they have
the gall to say their Orangemen Protestant colonists
are "superior and select"—a race apart!

                                        Like gods
the British deal out life to the one, death
to the other. It is a policy of murder, racial murder.

Not only is there the question of the "Anglo-Saxon" race.
We also have the "Caucasian" myth. I ask:
if the Caucasian race is so superior, how

did it happen a civilization flourished on the banks
of the Ganges thousands of years before the "Caucasian
race" climbed out of the mire of the Russian steppes?
I ask you, put yourself in the place of the Mexicans.
Imagine North America is yours. But then
the English take New York from you by force.
Next they tell you, "You are not Celts, exactly.
Nor are you Anglo-Saxons, or Goths, or Germans—
you are degenerates, an alien, bastard race."
And having told you that, they take away the state
of Massachusetts for good measure!

                      We Americans
have proved ourselves the true descendants of Saxons,
Danes, and Normans—yes, of all those ancient
ancestors whose offspring demonstrate a crapulous appetite
for someone else's land. In the past eight centuries
Englishmen descended from such races have taken
for themselves the lion's share of land on every
continent now lived on by the human family.
And we Americans bring the sins of our forebears
to ultimate perfection in Mexico! Ours is but
a single policy: race superiority
and naked aggression. It sends off some to prison,
dispatches others to the gallows, and forces thousands
into homelessness and poverty and despair. It is a doctrine for
       annihilation—
whether by the sword or by the workings of starvation
and neglect.

              Away with mawkish moralizing!
"Race" is a desecration of religion and political morality!
It is a serving-up of table scraps of dinner

speeches and club harangues in the mouths of idle
senators.

       I will not fall down, I will not worship
at the racial altar! I reject the craven cult
of Manifest Destiny. If we are to plunder
and dismember a sister republic, let us stand forth
like conquerors, and show our colors. We are the Spaniards
of our age. We go for glory. We go for gold.
We go for conquest, and to make men slaves!

July 1847

The Triumph of the Anglo-Saxon Race
and Manifest Destiny

Part II

The Susquehanna Philological Society of Philadelphia, Pennsylvania, herewith publishes the second of three installments of the spirited colloquy held in its rooms during April 1847 between the following noted medical and scientific personages: Doctor Charles White, Mister Phineas Cheveux, M.A., and Mr. Orson Fowler, P.P.

FOWLER: Doctor White has asked, "Do I wish to admit that the entire animal kingdom was originally derived from one single ancestral pair? " My answer is quite obvious: "Yes, of course. We are all descendants of our divine antecedents, Adam and Eve!"

WHITE: I said the entire animal kingdom! Adam and Eve would not be the ultimate parents in such a kingdom.

FOWLER: Oh? Who would be, then?

WHITE: Not who, what. For example, it could have been a pair of snakes. Yes, snakes mate in pairs, and they could be ancestors of ours just as much as any other pair of animals, could they not?

FOWLER: Ugh.

WHITE: Exactly. A more degrading notion cannot be entertained.

FOWLER: Agreed.

WHITE: So now are we not of one mind? The Negro, the American savage, and some Asiatics are, and must necessarily be, of different species from us. In fact, they are separate races, they are in no way related to us, and they are not descended from any ancestor common to us. Different ancestors, different origins.

FOWLER: You are persuasive, sir.

WHITE: Oh yes, Mister Fowler, I know that I am persuasive because what I say is quite true. The races may all be human, but mark this: we of the Anglo-Saxon race obviously are and must continue to be the prime link in the immense chain which extends to the lesser beings created around us. Of course there are those in each of the other races who are endued with various degrees of intelligence and with powers suited to their station. But we stand at their head. Do I take your continued silence as agreement on this point? Do you require further proof? Arrive in any foreign land, set foot upon its soil, look around you, and the contrast of what you see there with our intellectual achievements will immediately become apparent. And beauty, too. Where else will you find the nobly arched head containing such a quantity of brains save amongst our Anglo-Saxon people? Such a variety of features and fullness of expression—the long flowing ringlets of hair and the majestic beards. And in the females of our race, those rosy cheeks and coral lips? And the blush that overspreads their soft features, that emblem of their modesty and delicate feelings? Oh where, except in the bosom of the European woman, will you find two such plump and snowy white hemispheres so cunningly tipped with vermilion . . .

CHEVEUX: You've finished, haven't you, Doctor White? Doctor? Why is he looking off into space that way?

FOWLER: I don't know. Doctor White?

CHEVEUX: Doctor? We agree with you on the superiority of the Anglo-Saxon race.

FOWLER: And I know that we both share your enthusiasm for the fledgling science of ethnology. Doctor—are you quite all right?

WHITE: Ah? As I was saying, I am the only one here qualified to hold an opinion—

CHEVEUX: But now I want to talk about hair!

FOWLER: Yes, yes, we know that.

WHITE: Well, Mister Cheveux, tell us about your little hair collection.

CHEVEUX: Don't scoff.

WHITE: I didn't scoff.

CHEVEUX: Quite clearly your tone was condescending. Mine is not a "little" hair collection! The king of Saxony himself has entrusted to me a fine assortment.

FOWLER: Oh, for heaven's sake, man, get on with it.

CHEVEUX: Yes, very well. I shall begin with the hair of white men. It contains a microscopic canal for the distribution of coloring matter, a canal which is entirely lacking in the wool coming from the head of the Negro. Now, we all know by experience that of all animal pile, the pile of the head of the human male is the most highly and completely organized. Ergo, we may rank the hair of the white man as perfect hair. The wool of the head of a Negro, then, is imperfect hair. And what, you may ask, of the hair of mixed races and their descendants?

FOWLER: I take it from this that you regard hybrid offspring as capable of reproducing themselves?

CHEVEUX: Completely. The hair of the progeny of mixed races consists of filaments characteristic of each of the parent species—elliptical for the Negro, oval for the white. Thus, the hair of a mulatto is eccentrically elliptical and oval—partly perfect, partly imperfect. By examination I can determine the degree of racial hybridity of any given individual.

FOWLER: All very well, but what intellectual and moral attainment is shown in all this work of yours with hair canals?

CHEVEUX: Be patient, Mister Fowler. As I have said, I can determine the degree of hybridity of any given individual by examination of their hair. I have even drawn up a set of tables of hybridity for both simple and compound cases. I can assure you that despite Doctor White's assertions on this subject, the progeny of racial crossbreeds are quite fertile.

WHITE: The census of 1840 proved that in the state of Maine, mulattoes, for example—

FOWLER: The state of Maine is well hidden from the sight of God and the reach of science. I can still remember, in 1839 I examined some phrenological peculiarities of its rustic farmers—

CHEVEUX: Will you both be quiet? I want to talk about trichology, and you want to recount anecdotes about farmers in Maine. Now, under microscopic examination, the simple hybridity of black and white can produce seven degrees of hybridity of hair, namely: hepta-mulattin, hexa-mulattin, penta-mulattin, tetra-mulattin—

WHITE: Really, sir, we know the Greek lexicon. Come to the point.

CHEVEUX: As a result of my studies, I have concluded, first, that the ancient Egyptians were of the white race.

FOWLER: Now that is interesting.

WHITE: Are you quite sure?

CHEVEUX: Hair never lies.

WHITE: Except, of course, when the hair is lying on Mister Cheveux's head.

CHEVEUX: Doctor White, if you cannot dispute with me, I would request that you resist the temptation—

FOWLER: Mister Cheveux, if you please. Your first conclusion is quite interesting. Have you reached others?

CHEVEUX: My second conclusion is that the races are of separate origins. Each race constitutes an entirely separate species. I would especially point to the autochthonous origin of the American aborigines.

FOWLER: I see. Well, we seem to be approaching agreement on several matters. Any other conclusions?

CHEVEUX: One to which I would give special emphasis. Through my method, I have perfected a means to determine with exactness the racial origin and purity of any individual.

FOWLER: I had not thought such a thing was possible!

WHITE: I fail to see your drift.

CHEVEUX: In words of one syllable, certain persons present themselves in civil society, but their origins are questionable. In matters of state or commerce, or in any matter requiring absolute confidence, one must know everything about that person—even what he is least likely to admit to—do you understand what I mean? His race, gentlemen. If we wish to place our trust in him, we can know without question what a man's racial provenance is.

WHITE: You mean I snip off a lock of his hair and have Cheveux here look at it under his magnifying glass? It's an invasion of one's privacy, that's what it is. It's no damned business of anyone what the condition of my hair is.

CHEVEUX: Not yours, surely, Doctor White. But hypothetically—

WHITE: Hypothetically it will be some damned banker snipping away at me looking for an excuse not to extend me a loan. The principle of the thing is completely out of bounds.

CHEVEUX: On the contrary. For example, it could be of the highest importance to know the racial purity, say, of a future son-in-law. I have already acquainted our Senator John C. Calhoun with the possible applications of my discovery.

WHITE: I hope he has enough sense to light a fire in his grate with the paper it is written on.

CHEVEUX: Senator Calhoun has personally let it be known to me that he is giving it his most careful consideration.

FOWLER: Then I am sure your idea will find a champion in Senator Calhoun, even if most of the world knows him as the Great Nullifier. When I think of greatness in a public figure I think of Daniel Webster—

CHEVEUX: That tawdry New England politician!

WHITE: We are here to discuss science, gentlemen, not to winnow the grain on the political threshing-floor of the American Congress.

FOWLER: I was thinking only of the phrenological sciences when I mentioned the name of Mister Webster. He is a man with such a wondrous frontal-coronal development. In comparing his noble brow with that of a man of ordinary talents—

CHEVEUX: Senator Calhoun's brow—

FOWLER: Or for that matter, with the corresponding development of a Hindoo or a Chinee or an African or a savage American—we find that each one is a little smaller than the other, and at the end, the smallest is only a little larger than that of mere animals. I wish I had my charts here with me.

WHITE: Mister Fowler, we must be content to present our views in debate as best we can. Equal chances that way.

FOWLER: Well, I shall have to convince you without them. I have solid anatomical evidence that certain regions of our brain control our thought and our behavior. They are determinative.

WHITE: Then you must try as best you can, and see where it gets you!

Here ends the second installment. A final installment will be published in a succeeding number of the Acta.

September 1847

Brigham Young

There is a story being told at the eating and drinking establishment in this city presided over by Mr. Charlie Pfaff ("C. Pfaff's and die" is his motto). It is here retold, as relayed to us by Mister W. Whitman.

It seems that the Mormon pioneers, when they arrived at the place they now call Deseret, encountered an old "desert rat" who had been existing in a hand-to-mouth fashion for some time there. The old man had learned to live on almost nothing, and he found it wondrous that so many people could have braved so much to arrive in a place so unpromising for yielding them a living.

He marveled at the industry of the Mormons who promptly turned what had appeared to be a desert into a fruitful plain. But even more wondrous to him were the living arrangements of the Mormon men and women, and chief among them, their patriarch, Brigham Young.

It was inevitable that one day the old desert rat would meet Brigham Young and engage him in a conversation. This is the story, as the old man tells it:

"He lookt at me in a austeer manner fer a few minits. Then he sez 'Do you b'leeve in Solomon, Saint Paul, and the immaculateness of the Mormin Church an' the Latter-Day Revelashuns?" Sez I, "I'm on it!" (I make a pint to get along plesunt wif everbody, tho I didn't know what under the Son the old feller was drivin' at.)

"You air a marrid man, Mister Yung, I b'leeve?" sez I. "How do you like it as far as you hev got?"

"Middlin," sez he. "I hev got me eighty wives, sir."

"You sertinly air marrid," sez I.

"As you shall see!" sez he, an acordinly he tuk me to his Scareum. The house is powerful big, and in a exceedin' large room was his wives and children, which larst was squawkin' and hollerin' enuff to take the roof rite orf the house. The wimmin was of all sizes and ages. Sum was purty and sum was plane—sum was helthy, an' sum was on the wayne. "Besides these yere wives you see," sez he, "I have eighty more, in varis parts of this consecrated land, what air sealed to me."

Sez I, "Eighty *more*? You air a feature of the time, sir! Eighty air sealed to you?" sez I, starin at him.

"Sealed, sir, sealed!" sez he.

Sez I, "Whare 'bouts? Will they probly continner on in that fashun to any grate extent, sir, or will they be 'llowed to come out for air?"

"Sir," sez he, turning red as a biled beet, "don't you know that the rules of our Church is that I, the Profit, may hev as meny wives as I wants? Them as is sealed to me, that is to say, to be mine when I wants 'em, air at present my sperrytooul wives!"

"An' long may they wave!" sez I, seein I shoed get into a scrape ef I didn't raise Ol' Glory. "Sir, the female woman is one of the gratest instytooshuns of which this yere land can boste!"

And so the old man raised the flag and made his exit.

To this tale, our correspondent adds a footnote: "Brigham Young! A man who loves not wisely, but two hundred well!"

Gotham Magazine
New York
September 1847

Another Letter in Her Majesty's Diplomatic Pouch

To the Right Honourable Earl of Dunwoodie
c/o Ashburton and Williams, Solicitors
Gray's Inn
London
September 28, 1847

My Lord, and Gentlemen,

Lest the chronicles of our times lack for a truthful and precise history of the matter, I am most honoured to present to you, and to Her Majesty's commission regarding our contribution to the advancement of scientific knowledge in Her former American colonies, the following statement regarding my lifetime of scientific achievement.

As is well-known by every serious student of the matter, it was I who, as a young man, made the arduous journey from my native city in the British Isles to the valley of the Nile and the Pyramids of Egypt in order to conduct a thorough scientific investigation of those massive structures.

It was I who determined that their age was far greater than anything that had hitherto been allowed by those historians whose view of the matter had been limited by blind belief in the work of biblical scholars.

Since my arrival in the United States in autumn of 1837, it is I who have made the name of *Egypt* a household word in the somnolent cities of the American South.

It is I who then proceeded to awaken awe of ancient Egypt at every stage-stop and hamlet upon the American frontier.

As for Bishop Ussher's chronology of world history assigning the moment of creation of this marvelous and varied planet to the ludicrous year of 4004 B.C., I have set that fairy tale upon its head. I have brought back mummies from Egypt, I have studied them, and I have proved that both pyramids and mummies are far older than anything that Bishop Ussher could have imagined.

I have exposed my mummies to public view in New York City and in all the other centers of civilization in North America. What an impression they have made on a public which has numbered in the tens of thousands! For the price of a penny or two, the great mass of Americans has undergone an inestimably valuable educational and scientific experience!

I have contributed findings of vital significance to the founders of a new science named "anthropology." I have helped to found what is known as the "American school" of that science. I am the author of *Egypt: Illustrations Brilliantly Coloured, and Covering Many Thousand Square Feet of Surface.* It is a volume which may be found on the pianos, or on bookshelves next to the Holy Scriptures, in scores of thousands of American homes.

As a result of my indefatigable endeavours I have changed the mentality of the American populace. If many of them are now less committed to blind obedience to myths without scientific foundation, it is because of me. Before me, it was impossible to believe in a chronology of world history independent of the Bible. After me, it has been the only sane way in which to do so.

Before me, it was commonplace to believe in a single creation, Adam and Eve and the garden, etc. After me, it has been necessary to consider that there have been many creations, at various times, and over a period of scores of millennia.

Most important, it is now necessary to believe that the various races of mankind were each created differently, at different times and in different places in the earth's long history. Mankind is not descended from a single human ancestral pair.

As a result, if Americans are less committed to the glittering generalities of their Declaration of Independence—such as the dictum that "all men are created equal," etcera—then so be it: I am the cause of it.

I trust that this letter will ensure that proper attention will be paid to the work of one who has laboured long and faithfully in the cause of science in a distant corner of the world. I subscribe myself your most faithful servant and advocate of scientific advancement.

G. R. Glidden
Egyptologist

Mexico City Falls to General Scott's Troops!!

"The Greatest Military Achievement of the Modern Age!"

A Special Morning Edition of the *Sun*
A Revolution In News Reporting!

The following brief dispatch was one of a series brought as far as Charleston, South Carolina, by means of a steam packet boat engaged exclusively by our newly organized Associated Press service. From Charleston it was transmitted instantaneously to our New York offices via the telegraphic service established by Mister S. F. B. Morse. Additional dispatches will be published in full in these columns in our regular evening editions as soon as they are received either by telegraph or by the overland express.

M. Beach, Publisher
New York Sun

As of Tuesday, September the 14th, General Scott received the formal surrender of Mexico City.

Santa Anna has fled, our soldiers in blue are everywhere in the streets, and the fighting has ended!

The taking of Mexico City was not without cost. Furious resistance was encountered at several locations on the outskirts, and at the castle on Chapultepec Hill inside the city.

The total American force numbered just 12,000 men. Casualties are as yet unknown but are expected to be heavy.

However gallantly they fought, the Mexican troops were no match for American arms, artillery, and engineers, and most of all, our fearless spirit of enterprise.

Troops from every state and region shared in this brilliant military feat. All honor and glory is due to them, and to the architect of the invasion, General Winfield Scott.

It is certain that this triumph will lend such celebrity to General Scott's name as to make him the Whigs' candidate for president in our next election!

M. B., Jr.
September 1847

Mrs. Anne Royall's Pen Portrait of "The Price of Salt"

The typhus season is upon us once again. Every summer we citizens of Washington City suffer from the scourge and this year has been no exception.

In this period of enforced idleness I have been reflecting upon Mister Polk's current war with Mexico. A great many injustices have been noted in the causes and course of this conflict, but in general the nation's attention has been riveted upon the drama of General Scott's march from Vera Cruz to the Mexican capital.

As a remedy to the distractions offered by this war, I would like to offer my readers a pen portrait. But it is not a portrait of the war or of one of its heroes. It is of a thing. The thing is salt, and it is the true price of that common necessity, Kanawha County salt, which I shall paint for you in this pen portrait.

Every human being and every animal urgently needs salt in order to survive. At this time most of our salt comes from the Kanawha River area of western Virginia. How that salt is obtained, and how it is sold, is a story which you must know.

First, you have to seek out the places where common men and women earn their living. Their labor has a way of being kept apart, as if a veil should be drawn over it. And why? Nasty, dangerous things are done to laboring people where they work. Most of what they do is hard labor, and "hard labor" is not just a description of their work, it is a sentence. It is their doom.

The salty water needed for making salt is obtained from a second stream which runs deep beneath the bed of the Kanawha

River. They get to it by means of a thing they call a *gum,* which is a hollowed-out sycamore tree trunk, ten to twenty feet in length and four to five feet in diameter. They clamp an iron crow arrangement on the bottom, with a head that fixes it tight. They lay it in shallow water. Then about twenty hands take hold and the gum is lifted upright so that it stands on the crow end. A man is let down inside by means of a rope and windlass and he begins to dig around the inside edge of the gum, filling buckets with sand and gravel.

These are drawn up, emptied, let down again, on and on, and so the edge of the gum slowly descends down to solid rock. To pump out the water, a hand pump is let down inside the gum as the man works, but no man can stay inside for more than twenty or thirty minutes at a time because of the cold and damp.

For eight days and nights the work goes on until at last the gum rests securely on solid rock. Then a scaffold is erected over it. Now the men commence boring with an iron augur at two feet per day, sometimes up to 300 feet through that rock. That comes to a 150 days of back-breaking labor!

What a wretched appearance the poor creatures make when they are drawn out of that gum. They cannot stand up. They shiver as if they will shake to pieces. You can hardly tell if they are black or white, so completely chilled and purpled is their blood.

Now, there is not just one of these saltworks. There are mile upon mile of them, with hundreds, even thousands, of men working half-naked alongside horses and oxen that are beaten incessantly by their drivers, amid the smoke and fires of rendering tanks where the brine is converted into refined salt. What a mournful screaking sound of machinery, day and night, in a valley surrounded by gaunt, rugged mountains cut bare for their timber!

All this for a few cents a day in wages, under the thumb of bosses who boast of their skill in cheating the workers out of even that pittance!

We know the price those thieving bosses then charge our farmers on the frontier. For the salt they have obtained from the labor of those poor working men in Virginia, they charge the farmers one cow and one calf for each and every bushel!

These United States cannot remain free if one portion of its citizens is allowed to reduce our working-men to conditions of slavery and mercilessly to exploit our farmers. I say: seek out these places. See them, as I have seen them. Observe them carefully, and then you will know the price, the terrible price, we pay for Kanawha County salt!

Anne Royall, Editor
The Huntress
Washington, D.C.
September 1847

Flogging, Branding, and Bucking

We are not the ones to say that soldiers and marines
should not be punished. But today a young man paid
a visit to this office and showed the legacy of the *Colt*,
a rope with a double wall-knot tied at its end,
the navy's favorite whip. His back is a topographic
map of scars.

          Another case: a soldier
ran away because he heard his mother
died. Whatever the reason or the crime, nothing
can make us believe the raw, scarred "D" forever
branded on his cheek was justly due him. King George, perhaps,
or the ruthless Russian tsars, or even Santa Anna
might have done it. But not the army of the Republic.

Those are the punishments that leave their scars. One
other leaves no scars, but nonetheless,
"bucking" is inhuman. The offender sits upon
the ground, his knees drawn up to his chest. His hands
are tied in front of his shins. A pole is poked
beneath his knees, above his elbows. Pinned
in this wise, he is gagged and set out in the sun.

The Father of Our Country lost a quarter of his army
to desertion. Enthusiasm for our cause has meant far fewer,
a fraction of a fraction, will give the go-by to their duty.
Let us be firm, let us be just—but no more
medieval tortures for our soldiers and marines! Ours

is an army that would conquer a peace, and by God's grace, shall bring the blessings of freedom wherever it goes!

New Orleans *Picayune*
October 1847

A Quaker Prayer

Bring down, O Lord, this raping spirit that stalks
the land. That makes the people lose esteem
of Thee. That robs them of their meed of soul and body.
That takes away their countenance of modesty.
Their humanity. The tenderness of their persuasion.

Why should it be thus, seeing I
was never one to commit such evils? And the Light
of Christ revealed to me that it was needful
that I have the sense of all conditions of mankind.
How else might I speak to men of all conditions?

October 1847

A Prayer Offered in the
United States Senate

At the Convening of Its Sessions on December 6, 1847, by Its
Chaplain, the Rt. Rev. P. T. Bainum, D.D.

O God, Our God, Lord God of our fathers: we ask
Thy blessing and the favor of Thy grace on this sacred chamber.
Keep us mindful that now we are a nation among nations.
The workings of Thy providence decree our presence shall be felt.
The arms of this republic must needs reach out
to bear the fruits of liberty to other lands.
Yea, are we not required to do this? What
other nation hast Thou made worthy of the task?
Thou hast given us this government, one devised
to bless each citizen with equity and justice. We dedicate
its fruits forever to Thy name. We vow
our everlasting vigilance against the forces
of ignorance, depravity, and medieval tyranny. O Lord,
with Thy help, and Thy help alone, we shall be the victors!

Nevertheless there are the faint of heart who cry, "O Lord,
why hast Thou brought our nation to this place?"
The answer looks them squarely in the face. For a thousand
years the Lord has been preparing first
the Teutons, then the English-speaking peoples
for this moment. It is He who has commissioned us
to stand at the head of the races of mankind. We are not here
to pass our days in vanity and idle contemplation!

Mexico is ours! God has delivered this new world
continent into our hands!

Through the workings of His providence,
consecrated by the sister spirits of progress and enterprise,
this sacred chamber in its wisdom justly shall dispose
of the affairs of savage and senile peoples, as well
as of our own.

O Lord, Thou hast marked us with Thy mark! We
are Thy chosen people! May our work this day bring glory
to Thy name!

Great is the name of the Lord!

Amen.

1848

♦ ♦

To maintain that our successes are due to
Providence and not to our own cleverness is a
cunning way of increasing in our own eyes
the importance of our successes.

—CESARE PAVESE

♦ ♦

Men who pass most comfortably through the
world are those who possess good digestions
and hard hearts.

—HARRIET MARTINEAU

♦ ♦

A Creditor Announces the Sale
of a Collection

Six hundred Indian portraits, stored
in my warehouse.

Painted as a monument to a dying race—
Properly the possession of the American people—
Purchase them and cherish them in your duty to the future!

When it comes to the scratch, the people do not
always see fit to match their money
with the words of their mouths.

                        Make good on the chance
to honor the race that once possessed
the whole of this country and now is fast
fading before the tide of immigrants!

George Catlin is their author, and my debtor.

A bargain at sixty-five thousand dollars, the lot!

Joseph Harrison
Philadelphia *Weekly*
January 1848

A Memorandum to the President

Sir,

We have learned by telegraph from a newspaper correspondent friendly to our party that messages from Mexico are about to arrive on board a dispatch boat.

We have been informed by that same source that Mister Trist, the envoy you have so recently dismissed from his post in Mexico City, has used the several weeks between the time your order was dispatched and its arrival into his hands to negotiate a treaty of peace with the acting Mexican president, Sr. Peña y Peña. A copy of that treaty is on board the dispatch boat.

The treaty corresponds in all of its major features to the one you originally commissioned Trist to negotiate last year, including the $15 million indemnity to the Mexican government for loss of its territories in the Southwest, including California.

In the past days you have been besieged by Senators Douglas of Illinois and O'Sullivan of New York to take prompt measures to purchase the island of Cuba from Spain. Your secretary of the treasury is much in favor of this purchase and speaks of paying $100 million for it.

You also have heard much from Senator Hannegan and the zealous adherents of Mister Beach of the New York *Sun* that we seize all of the countries of the western hemisphere and incorporate them into the Union.

These schemes are physically and financially impracticable. They are the work of true believers who have proved themselves in the past to be undeterred by practical considerations of any sort.

I suggest that you discreetly let it be known to the Senate that the problems of the amalgamation of native peoples inherent in such schemes are so formidable that any consideration of our acquiring additional territories would sink this nation into a morass of race problems.

The peoples south of the Rio Grande are, in a phrase, colored, savage, and senile, and they will neither lend themselves to conquest nor simply fade away.

Merely by the weight of numbers they would certainly overwhelm our Caucasian stock.

Assert that if the treaty in its present form is ratified, there will be added to these United States a vast empire, the value of which in twenty years will be beyond calculation.

Of course, Senator Webster and the other Whigs will advocate that we take no territory at all from the Mexicans. They have long denounced this war and would like to see the treaty rejected— provided they can cast the responsibility for such an event on you and our party in time for the coming elections!

Once again, I remind you that no matter what your past course of action toward Mr. Trist has been, wise policy requires that you accept the treaty, and that you require the Senate to approve it.

The question of what to do about General Scott fades in importance beside it.

May I say that in a year, no one will remember the name of Trist. They will remember yours.

February 1848

The Triumph of the Anglo-Saxon Race and Manifest Destiny

Part III

The Susquehanna Philological Society of Philadelphia, Pennsylvania, herewith publishes the third of three installments of the spirited colloquy held in its rooms during April 1847 between the following noted medical and scientific personages: Doctor Charles White, Mister Phineas Cheveux, M.A., and Mr. Orson Fowler, P.P.

FOWLER: I shall now demonstrate that I have solid anatomical evidence to prove that certain regions of the brain control our thought and moral behavior. There are many of these centers, each with a discrete function, and each leaving its imprint on the outer cortex of the brain and the skull. Our European race, especially its descendants in America, possesses a much higher endowment of these centers and thereby of their corresponding faculties—more, actually, than any other portion of the human species. Hence the intellectual and moral superiority of the Anglo-Saxon race over all the other races.

WHITE: What does all this come to, exactly? Not an exercise in trichoschisis, I trust.

FOWLER: It opens up the door to additional distinctions, as between the Negro and the savage Indian. For example: in the Negro brain, the moral and reflective organs are of larger size in proportion to the organs of animal propensity in the Indian brain. The Negro, therefore, may be expected to be more docile, submissive, intelligent, patient, trustworthy, and susceptible of kindly emotions. He will be less cruel, cunning, and vindictive than the Indian.

CHEVEUX: One moment, sir. Do I hear you implying that there is even the slightest possibility that the institution of slavery might safely be abolished?

FOWLER: It is a scientific fact that the Negro possesses a very large moral and reflective tune, which inspires him with its day-to-day melody, even if his reasoning powers are smaller than ours.

CHEVEUX: Personally, I would not trust my personal safety in South Carolina to Mister Fowler's idea of a tune inside some field nigra's head.

FOWLER: Science is a test of one's sympathies, sir. One must be willing to accept new ideas even if they are at odds with one's prejudices.

WHITE: This notion of yours seems to leave the Indian pretty well out in the cold.

FOWLER: Let us just say that one must ever regard the American Indian with vigilance. His tune is feeble and intermittent. The small quantity of his brain in the coronal region must be compared with the immense development of his brain in the area of animal passions and selfish feelings. No, gentlemen, he can no more be made civilized than a leopard can change his spots.

WHITE: Lo, the poor Indian!

FOWLER: Of his race, we may say that it is run. Except for the Cherokee, whose cerebral organization for some reason is different. The animal portion of their brain is smaller and the reasoning portion is larger.

CHEVEUX: That is an anomaly, is it not?

WHITE: Can you discern a principle at work in that?

FOWLER: Only that the brain is an organ, and like all organs, it is susceptible of growth through exercise.

WHITE: You mean that brains can be made to grow and become stronger through a regime of systematic thought?

FOWLER: Yes. You see, gentlemen, I am an optimist. I see the possibility of improvement for all the races, within their stations, through the exercise of their brains. For moral exercise, give them the Christian religion. For instilling new concepts, mathematics and grammar. All of these will bring any number of salubrious influences to bear on the hitherto unused portions of their brains.

WHITE: All very well, Mister Fowler, but your approach, and your prescriptions of brain exercise, will prove to be intensely upsetting to the Christian population at large. They continue to insist that there was a common creation of all mankind from a single pair of ancestors. Adam and Eve, predestination, God's plan and all that, cut and dried. There is not much brain growth possible in predestination. And the Christian population is impervious to any reasoned argument on the subject.

FOWLER: Yes, yes, it is the old story. They simply cannot or will not understand that the study of natural history is given to us for a purpose other than discerning some obscure divine revelations.

CHEVEUX: Too true, Mister Fowler. The godly have become rude, even violent when I have undertaken to take samples of their hair for my investigations.

FOWLER: But surely rational Christians will look upon the biblical account of the creation as a mere allegory of events in the natural order.

WHITE: Rational Christians? That is a contradiction in terms.

CHEVEUX: And what about the abolitionist Christians? Brotherhood of man in Christ, etcetera. They are nothing but zealots.

WHITE: One or two of them have even charged that my scientific findings constitute a doctrine of "raciology." And why? Because I dwell upon differences between the races at a time when they are in the midst of a fight to abolish the slave traffic. Well, I have something to tell them. I have heard something convincing here today that was said by Mister Fowler, and now I am happy to affirm that I too can unconditionally condemn the slave trade.

FOWLER: Hear, hear!

WHITE: Because Negroes may be considered in principle to be at least the equals of thousands of Europeans in brain capacity, and therefore in moral responsibility.

CHEVEUX: What? Oh, never say that, never.

WHITE: Their brain, it is true, is inferior in size; however, this is the condition which currently obtains today under slavery. A greater exercise of their mental faculties in freedom will cause the Negroes' brains to grow. It is as you say, Fowler. Wholesome exercise will always favor the development of an organ.

CHEVEUX: What about those famous principles you so emphatically referred to a moment ago, Doctor White? Where is the principle in this? Are you saying that a change of this kind, which is really a change in habitat, will serve to permanently change the nigras' brains?

WHITE: No, I am not. And it is not a change in habitat.

CHEVEUX: It is. That is most certainly the implication.

FOWLER: Gentlemen, please. The hour is getting late. We have managed to agree on the superiority of the Anglo-Saxon race in regard to the other races, but with all the other issues that have come up we have not touched upon the related question which was to figure in our discussions, namely, the question of Manifest Destiny.

CHEVEUX: There are one or two other things I have been unable to comment on today. In my work, *Omnia Trichia*—

FOWLER: Alas, Mister Cheveux, we must conclude. Gentlemen, may we end our meeting on a note of unity? I do believe that some clarity has been achieved here, even given the divergence of our views and methods—

WHITE: I fail to see any scientific method in the work of this perambulating trichotomist! And I see it only accidentally in the work of a palpator of cranial protuberances!

FOWLER: Please, Doctor White, unity. I am saying that if we do not achieve it now, we shall do so later. Science is a great brotherhood, gentlemen. We shall continue to meet in the circle of its fellowship.

WHITE: That is as may be.

CHEVEUX: Not with the likes of you.

FOWLER: We shall, we shall, and I thank you both for your participation. Mister Cheveux, we honor your devotion to study and the exactness of your methods. It is an inspiration to all.

WHITE: He is a damned snooping nuisance.

CHEVEUX: That is offensive, sir. Prepare to accept my challenge!

FOWLER: Doctor White, remember, sir, that you are living in the United States. You are a guest in this country.

WHITE: I said that he—I mean his work—represents—is a grand and suitable continuance of science!

FOWLER: Thank you.

CHEVEUX: What did he say?

FOWLER: Before we adjourn, may I add that since I have come to this city of Philadelphia, the City of Brotherly Love founded by the Quakers, I have been amazed that so intense is the personal aversion of humane and educated Philadelphians to Negroes that they would no doubt shrink back from the gates of heaven if they were opened for them by a colored person.

CHEVEUX: Gentlemen, do you know it is only a short step from that observation of Mister Fowler's to an understanding of the doctrine of Manifest Destiny? Let me explain.

The record of the colloquy breaks off at this point.

February 1848

Mister John Quincy Adams
Enters His Dissent
on a Matter of Scientific Theory

"Ladies and gentlemen. You may class phrenology with alchemy,
judicial astrology, and augury. Let me remind you
that Cicero once said he wondered how two Roman
augurs could ever look each other in the face
without laughing. I too feel the same surprise—
that two learned phrenologists can meet and not
break into laughter!"

February 1848

Major Seb Simon Visits the President

Well, I got to Washington City and dropped in to the White
    House
and there was Mister Polk a-lookin' tired
as a rat what has been drawed through forty knotholes.
"Major Simon," says he to me, "I hadn't
thought to see you back from Mexico so soon!
How does things go there now? From the hero's-eye
perspective, I mean."

                Says I, "Sir, they hardly
goes on at all. Yer General Scott and General
Taylor both are red and angry as a pair
of boils to think you'd chuck 'em plump in the middle
of Old Mexico and not send reinforcements in to help 'em
keep the peace. Them Mexican guerrillas
will eat their little armies up."

                He closes
his eyes a spell. "Major Simon, this war
is of my own gettin' up, for my own use, and I
shall manage it just as I please. There is reason in all things!"

I thinks, "Now here's a real philosypher!" So I says,
"I do await the reason. I'm your man!"

Says he, "I never wanted Scott and Taylor
to whip the Mexicans so fast, 'specially when them upstart
generals both are Whigs and get the glory.
When I found that General Taylor was swellin' up

too big, I meant to stop him down at Monterey
and draw off part of his glory onto General Scott.
But Zack Taylor is a headstrong, dangerous man! He overstepped
his duty and blundered on to victory at Buena
Vista. That was a provocation what sot ever'thin' ablaze.
If that insubordinate lout had only let old Santa Anna
give him a handsome lickin' there we might 'a had
peace in a while, for I had my agents infiltrate
his lines—we might of wound up the business of this war
so's each of us had made a handsome plum
of the outcome! But no, that Taylor cut and slashed
his way to victory with just a handful of men.
Unlarned volunteers they were, and I'd thought
they'd be as harmless as a flock of sheep. But that blunder
of a victory of his poured all the fat onto the fire
and I have done the necessary. I relieved him of his command."

I'm fazed. "It's news to me! You mean, he's gone?"

"Gone. I sent him home. He's free to pursue
the thing he's always wanted, I mean, this orfice."
I thinks, "Damn, if that don't beat the Dutch!"
But I only says, "That surely is a stroke!"

He goes on. "But that's not all. General Scott
hasn't done much better. He licked the Mexicans too fast.
I determined early on that no one whip
the Mexicans full tilt, it wasn't prudent. All
the glory of this war fairly belongs to me
and I shall have it!" He pauses, then he winks. "I've spread
the toils onto General Scott. Relieved him of his command.
Ordered him up to trial for insubordination."

I'm beginnin' to feel that here's a man with birds
a-singin' in his head. But I only says to him,
"And how is that? He fairly is the hero's
hero!" Says he, "He is just another Whig
what wants to occupy this chair. I sent my Mister
Trist to Mexico to wind things up, but he also
showed himself to be too much the upstart.
I sacked him too."

              The pile of political corpses
is growin' by the second. I think it's time to calm him
down. Says I, "I'm sure I'd feel the same
if I was in your boots. You know, it seems a pity
you told the folks in Baltimore that you'd retire
when your first term is up. Why, you're so popular
you might well go for two, jest like Old Hickory!"

At that he gives me a tuck in the ribs and says,
"Major Simon, don't you understand? Tellin' 'em
I wouldn't stand another time is jest
another way to make 'em fierce that I
should do just that! Don't it ring a bell?
Caesar passed up the crown three times so he'd
be sure to get it in the end. Don't
you see, that's how Santa Anna works it
too. When he gets pretty near run down and shivering
in the wind and no place left to stand on, he'll send
his resignation in with a patriotic speech about
his leg and how he's lost it for Old Mexico,
and the people clamor to keep him in and cry out
'Viva Santa Anna!' And away he goes
and drums himself up an army and another term."

"Tellin' you the truth," he goes on confidentially,
"when I said all that in Baltimore I had some little
notion of retirin'. I'd found this Mexican War
a bother. But thinkin' twice about it, says I,
'There ought to be a way to make my enemies
take up a demonstration in my favor.' Patriotism, Major
Simon—it conquers all! I think I know just how
to write that ticket. And what a satisfaction
it will be!"

        With that he gives me a wink and a hearty
handshake. "I like your style," says he, "And by
the bye, I has a need for a aidy-campy
in a little matter I have pendin' with the Senate.
A hero like yerself could be a real
asset, if yer loyal. Air you loyal,
Major Simon?" The offer drops my jaw.
It flashes across my mind, "He thinks I'm worth
a go, and he don't know my real mind. The man's
as green as a cut-seed watermelon!" Sez I, "I'm a loyal
Democrat, I'm a real ripstaver—" "Enuf," says he.
"Yer on. Jest see my secretary as you go out."

February 1848

From a Music Hall

Cleveland is a goodly city to look upon
if you look upon it in the right direction.

It is Detroit, without frills.

February 1848

John Quincy Adams

1767–1848

On the bleak February morning of Wednesday the 23rd, after answering the roll call, Mister Adams toppled from his seat in the House and by the evening he was no more.

The quiet, venerable man, who, after serving as the sixth president of these United States, deigned to return to public life and serve the people of Massachusetts in the House of Representatives, is with us no more. In the continual uproar of the House, one could always identify him because of his peaceful and tranquil visage. And so he was, down to the end. In whatever capacity he served, he exemplified with dignity and reason a lifelong dedication to Whig ideals.

It was while the Senate was debating the treaty of peace with Mexico, ending the war he so

detested, that his life came to an end.

He was a man who knew his own mind. Let us remember him in the many sentiments which he has left behind as his legacy to us:

- That wherever general knowledge and sensibility have prevailed among the people, arbitrary government and oppression have lessened and disappeared, in proportion;

- That there is a determining principle in human nature which is founded on benevolence, and cherished in love. And justly so, for it portends the very survival of the individual—that is, the love of power. And the common people may thank it for their aspiration for independence, and for confining the power of the great within the limits of equity and reason;

- That all human beings have rights that cannot be repealed or restrained by human laws, for these rights are derived not from a human source, but from the great Legislator of the universe;

- That the earliest colonists transmitted to us, their descendants, a hereditary ardor for liberty and a thirst for knowledge, a fact which has made the makeup of the English peoples dominant in the new world;

- And that for this, we must ever consider the settlement of America with reverence and wonder—as the opening of a grand scene in the design of Providence for the illumination of the ignorant and the emancipation of the slavish part of mankind all over the earth.

National Intelligencer
Washington, D.C.
February 1848

The Valley of Chance

Notice to all members: in matters of personal honor
U.S. statute 1-28-1839
forbids the practice of dueling within the District.

Members of Congress are not exempt, no matter
the number of the terms of their tenure in this chamber.

There is a declivity a mile and a half from Bladensburg,
enclosed by two hills, at the base of which there runs
a small, reedy brook. Parties here
are hidden from the turnpike road. This is a place
that is said to be in use. The District line
runs through this vale, and parties from the District and Virginia
easily may pass over into Maryland and thus evade
the laws of their respective territories.

Nothing in this notice should suggest that any
of us condone an illegal and barbaric custom.
To the contrary, we think it bloody and disgraceful.

However, it continues. Members, be advised.

> Notice posted in the cloakroom of the House of Representatives
> March 1848

The Treaty

On the 10th of March at ten o'clock P.M.
the message came: the Senate had approved the treaty,
thirty-eight to fourteen, four abstaining.

Just two weeks after, the New York *Herald* gave out
texts of all my confidential messages.
Is there no way this government can keep a secret?

General Scott is abusive and malignant but in no
position to have known. It must be someone else,
close by. Someone in whom I placed my utmost
confidence.

        I am convinced the guilt lies with
the Cabinet. Yes—but who?

          ♦ ♦

        Withal, I have achieved
what I set out to do.

          ♦ ♦

        But now my strength
is failing. My associates are more and more in league
to use next year's election to their own advantage.

          ♦ ♦

There is a truth in this. He who would hold
the power and wield it must meet his end in exile.

        James K. Polk, *Diary*
        March 1848

An American's Tribute to a
Swiss Scientist Recently Arrived
at Harvard College

I am forever in the debt of Professor Agassiz.

                                                Prior
to his coming I believed the Negro was inferior.
Yet I was devoted to Mister Jefferson and his vision—
universal education, the injustice of the slave system.
But the figure of the Negro—inferior, yet demanding recognition
as a man and brother—seemed to block my way.

The words of Professor Agassiz cleared my brain.
I made a public declaration at the Jefferson Lyceum,
speaking to the question: "The Negro is not a man
within the meaning of the Declaration of Independence." What
the audience thought I would say and what I said
appeared incongruous. But truth is truth.

                                              Virginians
are hardly antislavery, to be sure, but
in speaking on this topic I touched a matter that their minds
had long kept hidden from debate. Simply put,
they had not thought the matter through: *The Negro
is not the son of Adam. He is a separate creation.
And since created separately, he has not felt
the shadow of depravity as Adam did. Wherefore
the need for Christian missions to the Negro?
Wherefore our concern to bring him up from sin,
save him, make him regenerate, when there is no need?*

Our race is the highest species, it reigns supreme.
By right we have the same dominion over
all the lower species, as with cows
and horses. But Negro servants moving through
our houses, cheerfully yielding unrequited
service, are constant proof we cannot rightly
derogate their race to degradation.

                    Each
of us inevitably must feel an overwhelming
sense of our inferiority in the face of their
demeanor. We must heed the signs. We must devote our lives
to witness to the meaning of these Negro-beings.

                    Thus
we are called to the cause of abolition—not because
all men are created equal, but because they are not!

                    The Reverend Moncure Conway
                    Letter to the Richmond *Courier Dispatch*
                    March 1848

The Intellect

"We believe in ourselves
as we do not believe in others.

"We permit all things to ourselves.
And that which we call 'sin' in others
is 'experiment' to us.

♦ ♦

"There is no 'crime'
to the intellect."

Ralph Waldo Emerson
March 1848

A Second Letter to
President James K. Polk from an
Overseer of His Plantation

Dear Sir:

nough i will write you a few lins   i receved youre Leter
dated 7th of this month   thare is won or two
of the feeld negros what is sick but on the mend   Old woman
Sarah dyed yestaday morn   got oup well
and was taken sick and dyed in 2 ours   the childurn
is sick wif hooping cof   heer is wot the dockor sey

◆ ◆

My dear Sir:

The children have whooping cough, Eva's child
will no doubt die in consequence of deep-seated
disease of the lungs. They have an affection of the throats
which is unattended with pain but of a fiery redness which spreads
suddenly and rapidly throughout the system and into
the lungs, the stomach, and the bowels, with excessive sweating,
collapse, and danger of speedy death. In the large
number of cases it is relieved by swabbing their throats
with Spirits of Turpentine or solution Lunar Caustic
and externally with rubefacients. I would call it Erysipelas
or Saint Anthony's fire of internal origin. Two deaths
have been in consequence of the sudden rise of Erysipelas
in all the organs. However, most of them have
sore throats, and with them, it does not get worse or spread.

M. Thomas

◆ ◆

thate is wot the dockor sey   wea have
a good deal of coten in the feld   paked 125 bags
have 25 in the gin house   I think wea will rase a plenty
of corn   I hev don as good as I no howe

I no you hev a nede for monny nau
you aire the presydunt an I respeck it

you kin bye frum Gen Gid Pillow
Harbert and his weif and chile and a boy name Jo
and a girl and another boy name Harrison
for purty cheap   we can use the extry hans

ole Harry the blacsmif sey he wish to bea
remembered to his mastr espshirly   hea sey hea be
your servent untill dath

                                        Yours respectfully,
                                        John A. Mairs

Beanland Plantation
Fayette, Mississippi

                                                    March 8, 1848

168

"Get Your Manes Out from Under Your Collars"

The times have laid a burden on so many of us. Were you to see him now, you would think Senator Daniel Webster much older, thinner, and sadder. Three weeks ago his son succumbed to the typhoid fever in the war with Mexico. The senator's fine-tuned voice and the moral fervor of his views have suddenly seemed to leave him. We ask: who, in such circumstances would have the stomach for a rousing speech to his colleagues in the sacred chamber?

As for us, we are having the usual difficulties in publishing this gazette. Now an additional one has been added. If push comes to shove, we may have to let Bill, our printer's apprentice, go, and I shall have to do the press work myself. Our readers know quite well that I have never considered myself to be demure, and at age 79 I still know how to take our old Ramage press apart and put it

back together. Nonetheless I do wish I did not have to do it. Bill is a pain sometimes, but he is coming around. That is the way of our young American working people. They say "no!" and sass you and find all manner of means to object to what you want them to do, but this is only because they have not yet had their manes pulled out from under their collars.

"Anne," my readers will ask, "what in the world are you talking about?"

The phrase comes from a pen portrait of mine dating from years back, and it has everything to do with how I think working people should be treated.

I am not a Quaker, but I have been around them a good deal, and I tell you, for all that people say that they look and act peculiar, I think they have truly taken the next step in understanding how we humans ought to treat each other.

There was a Quaker teamster, a black man who had once been a slave, whose name was James Osborne. He was a wonderful horseman and a log hauler. Now that is a brutal job for both men and horses. Usually the teamsters have great draft horses and they beat them, sometimes without mercy, especially when they are pulling logs up the slopes of hills.

One day this Quaker showed me his team. He had only a pretty gray and a bay, and certainly they were no match for a span of great draft horses. But when he would move logs he would say to his horses, "Now horses, this Quaker is going to put a little chunk of wood back of the wheels so as the wagon won't pull back on you. But first I am going to pull your manes out from under your collars!" Then he would lift their collars and get their manes out from under them, all the time talking to them, coaxing them and telling

how hard they would have to pull.

Then he showed me something else. He had fixed the single-trees where they pass into the doubletree with a heavy spring arrangement so that when his bay and his gray began to pull their load, that spring arrangement gave them a little relief and a little encouragement—a little "give" till they got into their pull. And all the while the other teamsters would be wielding their blacksnake whips to make their horses start right off on a dead pull, he would be touching them, and chocking the wheels, touching and chocking and coaxing, and you know, his horses did not have to get under their whole load all at once and pull it.

They got encouragement. That is exactly what it was, encouragement. And then, did they pull!

James Osborne said he was just doing for his horses what he believed his religion, what the

Quakers call their inner light, did for him. It seems to give relief, it seems to give encouragement. It seems to turn a job of cruel, hard work into a matter of loving cooperation.

If I have ever stood close to a man that I thought had a handle on the next step in how we human beings ought to be and how we ought to treat each other in the future, it was with my Quaker friend James Osborne, and his little horses that could work as hard as giants—and never got a beating in their lives!

Why cannot all Americans begin to do the same with each other?

Anne Royall, Editor
The Huntres
Washington, D.C.
June 1848

The Return of the Volunteers

Lud Jessup and the Widow

"Be keerful of widders. They's been the reasons for husbands
to stay to home, and even stronger reasons
for bachelors to go out." That's what I, Lud Jessup,
says, and you better set up and study my lesson.

We come back from the war and we was popular
with people what had said that we was nothing
more than a bunch of yellow suck-egg dogs
the year afore. Once you seen Old Mexico
and done fandango dancin' and been rumsquaddled
with aguardenty and took a shot or two
at the recedin' green and white and red of Santy
Anny's britches, comin' back to hometown life
'pears to be all mud and soogans and screwn
up Methodizers. Whar, o whar, is she—

   The Spanish maid with eye of fire
   What at balmy evening turns her lyre
   And lookin' to the eastern sky
   Awaits a Yankee's chivalry?

There's only Betsy and Ulva and Susie and Myrlene,
and dancin' ain't allowed.

                  Old Miz Inchly
wore shiny specs. Round, shiny specs. If ever

you see some gray hairt woman behind a pair
of shiny specs jest keep yer eyes peeled, she's
dangerous in the extreme. Bet on it! No tellin' what
she'll do. Miz Inchly kept the buzzards from cheatin'
the worms for years, she did. When she died her heart
jest stopt a-beatin'. Why? Because she lost
her prize nine-di'mond quilt, that's why. I mean,
it's true a skittery hoss ran over her along
the way, but she'd a got over that if'n the nine-
di'mond quilt hadn't got all stomped on. Quilts
was her special gift—Irish chain, star-
over-Texas, sunflower, saw-teeth, checkerboard,
shell, nine-di'mond—the whole kerboodle! Go
to her house, they was packed away in chests, layin'
on the shelfs, hung four-double on clotheslines in the loft,
piled onto chairs and even onto the beds four-deep.
She gave 'em away at weddings. Fat Sal, for instance.
Got married, got a pile of quilts from Miz Inchly.
I ask you, what is a fat gal like Sal a-goin'
to do with twenty layers of quilts layin' on top
of her in the middle of July? Yaw! I'd just
as leave be shut up in the boiler room of a four-
deck steamboat with a three-hundred pound bag of lard as make
a business of sleepin' with that gal! It's obstinaciously cruel!
Howsomever, quilts don't get made all by theirselves.
Miz Inchly'd let the word go out that Saturday
she'd be quiltin'. "Three quilts and one comforter to tie,
and gobblers, fiddles, gals, and whisky." She'd send
that out to menfolk, and never a more tetchin' nor wakenin'
word were sent offen a woman's tongue. Then
she'd go to the gals and say, "Sweet toddy, dancin',
huggin' and huggers a few." Them words would strike

into the pit of the stomach of a gal and spread a ticklin'
all-ways-runnin' until them gals would scratch
their heads with one hand and heels with the other.

And sure enuff, ever'body's there except
the constable and the circuit-riding Methodizer,
what I'd say were two nobody missed at all.
Always a few more boys nor girls come there
what makes it more excitin'. It gives the she's
a chance to kick and squeal without the risk
of gettin' kissed at all. And it gives some grounds
for scrimmages among the he's. What I say,
good quiltins' with good free drinkin', good free eatin',
good free huggin', good free dancin', and good
free fightin' really huzz the fuzz.

                          This time the she's
had got there early and the he's arrived towards sundown.
Soon as they did, the needle-drivin' lost
ground fast, threads begun to break and thimbles
wandered off. They was gigglin' and winkin' and whisperin'
and smoothin' hair and ticklin' one another.
I'll tell you this, it ain't the gals and old maids
what are the ones to fool away your time on.
Widders, them's the ticket. There is lots of 'em now
what with the *vomito* and typhoid fever down
in Mexico—their men gone off but never come
back. So here they are, they's widders, and they's
sensible, steady-goin' never-skeerin',
never-kickin', willin' pacers, yes
they are. One will come up close and stand there
with her purty silky ears and her neck-veins throbbin',
waitin' fer the word. Which of course you gives, once

you got yer feet well set in the stirrups. Then away
she moves like a spring-buggy runnin' in damp sand. Give me
a willin' widder—what they don't know ain't worth
the learnin'. They been to Jamakey, they learnt how
sugar is made. As fer me, I found myself
a certain twenty-five year-old with round
ankles and bright eyes what was honestly lookin' into
mine and sayin' as plain as a partridge says,
"Bob White! I has been there, and you know it. And if you has
good sense, there'll be no use in humbug—no use
in a borrowed hoss, no use in hair-dye, no use
in cloves to kill your whiskey breath, no use
to buyin' closed curtains for your bed. I has been there!
I am your special providence. I am for ripenin'
green men, I am for killin' off the weak ones,
I am for makin' the sound ones happy in eternity.
Now come ahead!"

       There she was. But they
was a crowd of men around her like at a nickel
auction. I says to myself, "Time to stir
the pot!" They was one partic'lar feller out
from town, a red-combed, long-spurred specymin
with a red and white gridiron jacket and patent
leather gaiters. You knows the kind. He's brought
a hoss he's special proud on, a wild, scary,
wall-eyed devil. He's tied him to a cherry limb.
I thinks, if that there hoss could cotch a scare
big enough, he'd run like Jehu all the way
to town and then some. If I could only tetch him off.
Then I sees Miz Inchly's clothesline. There's nine quilts
hangin' on it and it's tied to the selfsame cherry tree!
So I rigs the clothesline to the hoss. And then I gives him

a whack with a palin' from out the fence and right about
nine inches off the root of his tail, I mean
so hard my hands begun to tingle and I busted
that palin' into splinters. I falls right over when old Wall-eye
tears down that limb with a twenty-foot jump, takin'
the line of quilts along. He heads straight out,
but not for town. He's runnin' for the house!

That's where he comes athwart Miz Inchly. She's holdin'
her nine-di'mond quilt, it's all spread out so she
can see it close, and then the damned unmannerly
fool of a horse run over her from behind. He stomps
his front hoofs plumb through her quilt and takes it along
with all the rest, runnin' and kickin' and causin'
them quilts to crack like flags in a breeze. The she's
is a-screamin' and the he's is hollerin' "Whoa!" and old
Miz Inchly is limber as a wet string now. Old
Wall Eye takes a turn around the parlor.
His line of quilts commences takin' out the bric-a-brac.
Now the she's begin to run so he heads
for the kitchen door and throngs right in. There is a crashin'
of pans and crockery and then he exits out
the back door like a ancient war horse trailin' paisley
armor. Miz Inchly moans out, "Oh, my precious
nine-di'mond quilt!" And cashes in her checks.

Burn my skin if Old Wall Eye doesn't streak
toward town with the feller what had brought him humpin' along
behind, his gridiron jacket lost to sight amongst
the disappearin' quilts, and leavin' us his nine-gallon
hat and a pair of gloves and a jack of hearts
on the playin' table. As he disappears I sees
my pretty little widow with nice round ankles

lookin' straight at me. There's just a slice
of a smile that's formin' at the corners of her mouth. Yaw!
I tell you, what a widder don't know ain't worth the learnin'!

But there it was, old Miz Inchly wasn't
comin' back. The constable and the circuit-ridin'
Methodizer got a bill what they have posted for my arrest
and I'm long gone from there. And where is she,

    The Spanish maid with eye of fire
    What at balmy evening turns her lyre
    And lookin' to the eastern sky
    Awaits a Yankee's chivalry?

And where's my steady-goin', never-skeerin',
never kickin' pacer?

              I'll tell you where.
Gone. Forever. And why? Because Miz Inchly
would have rather die than see her quilt displaced
one inch, no matter how. So much for bein'
a veteran of the war. Comin' home is mud
and soogans! And that's the obstinacious truth!

July 1848

July 4, 1848

This day having been
                appointed for the laying
    of the cornerstone of the Washington Monument,

and having been
                invited by the committee of arrangements
to attend,

and having determined,
                though in feeble health, to do so;

and accompanied

                by the Cabinet and escorted by the Marshall of
the District,
and by a troop of horse, and in the finest of carriages;

I therefore
            moved with the procession from the City Hall
to the banks of the Potomac,

and there the cornerstone was laid.

                        I thereupon returned
to the President's House and then reviewed a long
and colorful parade of dragoons on horseback.

◆ ◆

Later Doctor Rayburn came by, bearing
the treaty — ratified by the Mexican government.

                                        It is done.

I say that there is no such thing as fate
that falls on a man who fails to act.

                            But there
is a fate that falls on a man unless he acts.

Old Hickory said: "One man with courage makes
the majority."

                    So will the chroniclers speak of me!

                                        James K. Polk, *Diary*

Another View of the Washington Monument

The Corner Stone of Genral Washintons monument
wher lain by Hon James K Polk the presydent
tuesdy forth July and they wher great
prosesions, diferent volunters and United
States draggones and battrys flying artilliery

guvners of states and teritorys and sentors
and repasentives wher present, the mayo of the city
and alldermen and ecsetry   it wher a splendid day
and everthin went on peacebul and quite
and they wher a great display of fier works
but the Stone dudnt git to wher it be by magick
all the Mechanic and laberors of Washinton navy
yard hed volinteer ther selves to carry it
over to the tune of hial Columba and yankee doodle
and mister mills he say it be the next

millenum befor thay finish it ereckshun
I no I feel sum proud in thiss I wher
a slave and nau Ime free and I kin rite
and I kin work and have dun my part like any
man and I sai,

    peace and harmonny for al.

          Michael Shiner, *Diary*
          July 1848

From Margaret Fuller's
Italian Journal

Rome

My baby Angelino is three months old. He
is with his nurse in Rieti, where there is peace.

My husband Giovanni is somewhere, I know not
where, fighting with Garibaldi's legions.

The struggle for a Roman republic grows more murderous
by the week. What sense had I of this two years ago—
that I would not be in London, in the galleries, but at
the barricades of a bloody revolution?

◆ ◆

I have thought again of father. In my tenderest years,
before I went to sleep, I would read the books
he ordered. Something heroic—the Aeneid, let us say—
and that night in my dreams I would be in a forest where the trees
grew thick around me. But they were dripping blood!
And I would be walking with such intensity, but I knew not
where. To arrive was all my purpose. As I made
my way the blood kept dripping slowly from the trees
until it came to be a pool, at first
a shallow one, but at a certain moment my eyes
looked down and I beheld its color. Rubylike.
Fascination overcame me. My steps grew slower. Now
the blood was covering my ankles. The pool was rising
higher, and suddenly I could smell it. It was warm, it was rank.
It was the stench of the slaughterhouse, of the iron cauldron

of blood pudding reeking on the Christmas hearth, but so much
sharper that my stomach heaved. And then I felt
the blood, yes, felt it, warm and rising past
my thighs, my waist, my elbows, then my shoulders
till it touched my chin and then my lips!
I had come to the chamber of death! What could I do?
I prayed the first and only prayer of my life—
O give me truth! Cheat me by no illusion!

♦ ♦

Life is not a dream, now. Blood is real,
death is real.

♦ ♦

New England was a dream of piety,
and only a dream. There, I stood upon
the brink of knowing, but never learned to see
this life.
            Now I can see, can hear, and what
do I behold? The coils of something once
invisible to me are now as real as rock:
history, hard, determining history, the force
that makes us dance like puppets on a string.

♦ ♦

                                                Once
I held a Conversations class in Boston.
I lectured on the gods and goddesses, and on the great Disparities.
I have come far from what I taught back then—
that women are predilect in truth and sensibility.
Now I see another way of being.
It leads one down and down. One must be
prepared to move from dark to greater dark.

♦ ♦

To see the history-puppeteer, one has to see the word
"society." It is a word whose face had once presented me
with images of loved ones.

                        It has another face.
Society is not what we would like to see.
It is what is there—not as something we intend
but something much more ominous. Cold and vast
and ominous. Something we do not intend. As if
a force beyond our private wills had had its way.
New England taught that a walk in the woods and simple
piety were ends enough to live by, and heaven knows
one cannot live without the comfort of such interludes.
But in the sinews of time, in the flexing of our corporate
selves, such moments only come and go.
No walks in the woods, no simple pieties, in Rome.

                        ♦ ♦

The revolution. What began with crowds
and demonstrations and manifestoes has ended up
in bloody siege, betrayal, counterrevolution.

I still dream of blood. But it is Giovanni's now.
I see a hospital, a place where the wounded
come on carts, on stretchers, on the backs of half-starved
mules in a swelling, bloody tide. And the wounds!
The cannon wounds are worst—great gaping holes,
the flaming colors of the inward parts exposed.
The rifle balls are hardly better, they break
the bones, bringing on gangrene. Now I can see it—
the olive-green and black, the rotting smell,
the ones with fever, and those who come in rigid,
the pupils of their eyes so set on distant things,

never to speak or even hear your voice.
I fear my own dear husband may be one of them.

Bandages. Bed linen. Bed pans. Dressings. Trays.
And then—it is as if one looks at them anew,
these suffering men, what is left of Garibaldi's legions.
So many amputees, so many dying.
Could I sell the hair from my head or the blood from my arms
I would do anything for them, anything!

◆ ◆

Suddenly I saw them in a different way. Oh the men
were suffering there around me, no change in that,
but what they were had changed. I saw them now
as a vast and ravaged class. Their dream of liberty-
or-death had only served to hide from them
another, more important thing, something
neither they nor those who were their leaders saw.

Their leaders talked of politics, but never economics.
The liberty that they fought for was a dream, not a bad thing
in itself, but just a dream the leaders showed them,
cleverly, while economic bonds of class and privilege
held them prisoner.

◆ ◆

They count eight pigs of iron to make
one fodder. They count eight drafted soldiers to make
one squad. It all adds up. And so this thing that makes
us dance, this legendary puppeteer,
whose twitching fingers hold the cords controlling
us, is counting. And the world explodes with greed!

◆ ◆

How many times we think of death, only
to come to see there is but one true death.

Then, and only then, our eyes are opened!
Pity instead the man who can only live
as well as he knows how. It seems to him if he
were free he then would feel the more forlorn—
he sees the charm, the nobleness of that free life,
but knows not how to live it. It is the element
to which his mental frame has not been trained.
In fact, he knows not what to do, today,
nor what, tomorrow; nor how to stay by himself, how
to meet others, how to act, how to rest,
and he cries in despairing sadness, "Why, oh why,
Father of Spirits, did'st thou not enlighten me?"

He is bound by the thousand chains which press on him
and make him captive of himself.

                              If he but thought,
"The life of the plant, no less than the life of each of us,
cannot be defeated! We must scatter our seeds
again and yet again until at last
we come to perfect flower. A choice can never
be too late, and though a moment's delay
against conviction is of incalculable weight,
the mistakes of forty years are but as dust
on the balance held by the great unerring hand!
Despair is for time. Hope is for eternity."

July 1848

A Debate in the Senate

I have always regarded those who burn to tread the Oregon Trail as evangelists of a lost cause. I am glad to see you go: Godspeed to those worthless faraway regions of the West, which the British parted with so willingly! I pity the poor Indians who must suffer your incursion, and I pity all of you for the long insidious arms of the "land gamblers" who will always grab the best properties early. As for rest of us, we are left with false inducements, raids on the treasury for a standing army, money for ports and customs houses—all for a turn of the cards three thousand miles away!

This time, though, with Oregon, the president has taken land through peaceful means. The British have seen fit to draw a line acceptable to all, and there the matter ends. But not the question—will Oregon be slave, or free?

And so it was that Mister Webster rose to speak to the Senate. At first you would have thought him older, thinner, sadder. As our readers know, three weeks ago his son succumbed to typhoid in the war with Mexico. How could the senator have the stomach for a speech?

He started slow and feeble-like. His fine-tuned voice and fervor seemed to sag. But when it came to the spread of slavery, his old strength seemed to flare, his words enkindled color in his cheeks and lent a power to his voice that would not be denied. He galvanized the galleries filled with partisans of both persuasions! He turned the tide, and won the day!

Mister Calhoun now must needs nurse his wounds.

Oregon may be no prize—but it will be free!

Anne Royall, Editor
The Huntress
Washington, D.C.
August 1848

The Evacuation of Our Troops

We are informed by our correspondent on the scene that the evacuation of American forces from Mexico is now in full sway.

Many volunteers had already been dispatched some time ago. Now it can be said that all forces, volunteer and regular, will have departed Mexican soil by the end of the month.

For tactical brilliance, the achievements of General Taylor and General Scott will withstand any test that history may see fit to apply.

However, the president has recently pointed out that the greatest achievement of this war has been to demonstrate that a republic such as ours can undertake an invasion of a foreign power with all the vigor normally belonging to the autocratic forms of government to be found in Europe.

In addition, the record of our achievements in this war makes it clear that our republic can never be charged by future generations with want of unity or concentration of purpose or failing to prosecute the vigorous execution of a war by citizen soldiers. Our republic undertook a campaign against a military despotism masquerading as the "Mexican Republic" and has conquered a just and durable peace. Surely now it can be said that we are a nation among nations!

The cost of this war to us has been greater than many had anticipated. It is thought that the number of our dead total more than ten thousand, with an equal number who died of disease during the period. The financial burden has no doubt exceeded initial estimates, perhaps amounting to one hundred million dollars. But the United States has enlarged its territory by almost one-half, and the Western Commonwealth is ours!

Our prophecy regarding *Manifest Destiny* has come true. Our nation's soul sought a celestial beacon. It was found. And we have been guided into a future worthy of ancient myth!

United States Magazine and Democratic Review
August 1848

John Charles Frémont, on
His Fatal Expedition

October 1848. Court-martial
ended. All that is behind me now. I have a new appointment,
my struggle to redeem myself is just beginning.

I am almost forty. What have I got to show
for all my years of labor? Only my maps,
a gold-mounted sword, and a seven-hundred-thousand-
dollar debt. But there are a hundred million
acres of wilderness out west. No end to it, ever!

The face of the earth is my calling. There has to be
a right-of-way across the Rockies for a railroad.
I take a party out from Kansas. But I ride
the ten miles back to camp to have a final
hour with Jess, my dearest. Her maid gets up
to make a pot of tea for a stirrup cup.
But all the while I think of mountains—they seem
to loom before me, lowering on the horizon, wrapped
in snow. No sooner do we leave our Kansas camp
than a blizzard sweeps down upon us. By Bent's Fort
the snow is shank-deep to our animals as they labor
into the stockade. And the nights—they are like the waters
of some dark sea where little phosphorescent stars
will bubble up, shine for a moment, and disappear
in the aching chill above. And then, at last,
the snowbound Rocky Mountains, white as tombs,
licked at night by tongues of the aurora borealis.

When we plunge into the defile at Hard Scrabble
it is one continuous snowstorm. A Canadian says,
"I don't want my bones to bleach upon
these mountains, sir!" "Turn back, or forever
hold your tongue," I shout, and he turns back.

There is a moment on that eastern slope when you can look
below you, backward, downward, outward, at the great
expanse of plains you have left behind. There
they are, a placid sea, and everywhere the snow
a massive spume that covers them, catching
the setting sun with bursts of iridescence, with a faint
calligraphy of streams and outcrops showing through.
And as the sun sets, how those bursts turn into welcome signals,
mirrors flashing "Come down! Come home!" through the slowly
purpling air. As you turn your face back toward
the Front Range of the Rockies—the sun gone down behind it
now—dark with ice and timber, one peak indistinguishable
from another— through the notches of the passes
we have put our hopes in so completely
you see the moiling tops of storm clouds
filling the defiles, until it seems the whole
of what lies before you is one long darkening rise
to peaks that shroud themselves and everything
beneath in a continual maelstrom of winter storms
and snow.

It is the moment when all the others
want to turn their backs on you and hearken
to those mirror-signals from the plains. But for me,
it is the most beautiful of moments—when I make
my body turn toward the peaks with a certainty
that I can, I will prevaii! That I will find

my way through all the homicidal bluster of those storms
by the quickness of my wits and the coldness of my calculation.
My determination to conquer winter
storms requires not heat but something icier
than nature ever knew, or ever will!

It is winter, deepest winter, and the peaks are always
there. But there is no light, no sun, no banners
are in our train. Only that pall of snow, the wind,
the rigors of the cold.

               I have to rely on a man,
Bill Williams, a mountain man who proves
never to have known, or entirely to have forgot, the whole
of the country we are passing through. Here it is,
December now, and Williams keeps insisting
he knows every inch of the country better than I know
my own garden! He tells me this while on a ragged
track a handsbreadth away from an abyss, in gorges
lost in mists and bitter winds and hail,
with towering banks of rocks, sheer cliffs of stone,
and a trail made slick with a driven cap of sleet
and ice! In between the roar of the gale
and the gasps of your breath you hear the sudden scrabble
of mule shoes on rock, then a shrieking bray
as a mule with its precious packs goes rolling to the bottom.
"Retrieve the packs!" I order. I will not tolerate
the slightest lethargy.

               We come to a rushing stream
in all that ice and rock. Its bed is rough
and boggy, and some of the animals begin to balk
as we belabor them, waist-deep in that bitter stream.

Then having shoved and hauled them dripping up to higher
ground, we find them frozen stiff at dawn.

We begin to slow, ourselves. Williams drops
off his mule. We haul him back to camp,
cut him off his saddle, and warm him back
to life.

We toil in the terrible grip of snow sleep,
slow to break the warming seal of blankets
in the morning, slower still in labor, with the rising
sense that we must stop, lie down, give in
to a sweet—I know not what—torpor. At a certain
point, Bill Williams challenges me. "We go left!" he cries.
"My calculation is to the right!" I counter.
We go right.

The others always marvel
at how I know to make such quick decisions.
I always know. My instinct. But all the while
our animals are getting ravenous, sleepless
with hunger, abandoning our camps, breaking
their tethers, devouring rawhide lariats and the blankets
we throw over them at night, even
their manes and tails. Finally, when we rise to march,
the weak ones start to flounder, and we with our fingers
cut and bleeding have to free them, lift
their packs, haul them to their feet and rig
their packs again. I drive them on, and so
it is in Christmas week we find ourselves
on the gray and treeless spine of the Great Divide.

I force my men to try to cross the pass.
The storms are now unceasing, the dry snow blows
in gales so thick that you can neither see
nor breathe. The mules are lying down to die
around our fires. I give the order to make mauls,
and we beat the snow until it takes our weight
so we can pitch our camp below the timberline
again. Our trail is that of a defeated army,
dead animals and packs and empty saddles. And then
the blizzards come upon us once again.
We are at twelve thousand feet. It is impossible to go on,
impossible to turn back. That being the case,
it comes to me—a sense of resolution
even beyond the one I felt before,
back on the eastern slope. It is a matter
of calculation, and it comes from my deepest self.

It gives my heart both ease and comfort: I go back,
I recalculate my plans, I even take
a day to read from Blackstone's *Laws* and others
from a favorite shelf of books I have brought along.
Bill Williams is astonished, furious. "Reading?"
he keeps shouting, "Reading? Now?"

It takes two weeks to move our camp a half
a mile. No food, no animals. We're half-blind with snow.
Our fires burn into pits a dozen feet
below the surface. Williams says we have reached
our final point—"The Frémont Cemetery Butte."

I divide the men. Williams and a group
of three I send back down the way we came,

thence to the nearest settlement in New Mexico
for food, before returning for a rendezvous
again with us. The rest of us try for the Rio
Grande. But though we are on the downward path
the winds blow even colder now. We boil
our parfleche and rawhide ropes into a kind of gruel.
Scarcely a mile a day we make.

                    Then one
of the men lies down beside the trail in snow sleep.
We never bury him. We eat the bones a wolf
has gnawed and left behind.
                     At last, when we
have reached our rendezvous, there is no one there.

I take a pair of men to go to search.
"Work and save the baggage!" I tell the others,
"and if you want to see me again, you'll have to hurry—
I'm off to California!" So many times
I am asked, "Why the order to the men
that they at all costs save the baggage?" I say
it is obvious—my surveyor's instruments, my records!
And my Blackstone, don't forget! But those
words of mine have hit a nerve. They take it
that I had cut them loose in a rash and headstrong change
of orders. I say they are wrong, but they are unconvinced.

It is on the sixth day that we find the other party.
Only three remain.
Old Bill Williams is a skeleton, the other two
are little more. Of the fourth they will not speak,
but in time the charge is made that they have eaten him.

Kit Carson always said, "In starving times,
a smart man never walks in front of Old
Bill Williams."
                    You have no idea what comfort to the soul
it is at last to lie in bed in Kit Carson's
house at Taos, be served a cup of chocolate,
and touch the spine of my beloved Blackstone
once again. These are the moments to remember
for the Pathfinder, when his greatest danger and fatigue
have passed. But the others, when they hear of what I have done
they say they never will forgive me. That to save
a miserable box of British books, I ordered
them to offer up their very lives!
They never took account of the cruel persistence
of misfortune, nor of all the precautions that I tried to take,
nor of all the monumental bad advice I got.
They see me now as petty, and as tyrannous.
As a mere trifler.

                    There is something here inside me,
something that excites the admiration of so many,
then repels it. That inspires such an image
just in the telling of my deeds, and then begins
to tear it down. It is as if I am a kind
of monument, always in the hands of an indecisive sculptor.

                              John Charles Frémont, *Diary*
                              November 1848

Major Seb Simon on Tour
with the President

Well, we got to Quaker City and they took us
up to a hall was bigger than a meetin' house.
No sooner there, the folk commenced to pourin'
in by the thousands just to shake the Presydent's
hand! There was such a stream a-comin' that the hall
was full directly, I mean, it was so hell-to-breakfast
full a fella couldn't get a leg-and-arm
outside the door again, was he to die!
We had to knock the windowglasses out
and let them go out thataway. Jimmy Polk
shook hands with all his might for a hour or two,
then he got so tired he couldn't hardly stand.
I says to myself, "If I'm his aiddy-campy
I'll just step in and take ahold and shake
for him awhile."
            Soon he's so exflunctified
he lays down on a bench that's covered with a damask cloth
and continners on, shakin' away as best
he can. And when he couldn't shake, he'd just
nod to 'em as they come along. At last he got
so beaten out the best he done was wrinkle up
his forehead. Or wink. That was when I scrunched
myself behind and reached my arm around
on top of his and shook for him for just
about a half a hour as tight as I could spring.

He 'jerned the session for the day and went to take
his ease in a room next door. He asked for me

to set with him a spell. "Sir," says I,
"back home I'm mostly in the apple trade. Have been,
since my youth. But I don't care that much about
the apple line, I've found a way to get rich
quick that's more than forty times fast-movin'
than any apple biz."

              He sot right up
and laughed. "And what is that, my friend?" he asks.
"Sir," I says, "now that we are closeted,
I'll tell you some. Just go directly home
to Tennessee, for there's a enterprise a-goin' on
out there where you get rich about a hundred
times more fast as bein' Presydent! I mean,
you only get your five-and-twenty thousand
per, but in that there business you can pull down five-
and-twenty in a week if your a mind to. And not
work hard at all!" "Major Simon, tell me
what it is!" says he. I can see that he's
commenced to feel rather in a pucker about
my scheme, so I says, "You must keep this to yourself. If all them
Washington toadies and congressers come onto it
and start a-dippin' into it they'll cut us out."
"You kin bet your bones on that," he cries. So I
goes on: "You see, it's nothin' more nor less
than sellin' land. It's forty times more fruitful
than diggin' with a hoe. You need a Mormon-size
passel of relatives, startin' with your uncles."
"I'm with you there," says he, "I got two loads of 'em."
"So," says I, "your Uncle Simon buys
a piece of township back of Millyville and
gives a note—three thousand, say—to the bank.
He sells it then to Uncle Josh for four

197

who gives his note to Uncle Si; Josh
sells it then to Uncle Zack and takes
his note for five; and Uncle Zack then sells it
off to Uncle Jim and takes his note
for six; then Uncle Jim to Uncle Mac
for seven. Uncle Mac then pawns it off
on Billy Johnson, and he takes his note for eight.
So there they are, five uncles not worth six
bits apiece for starters, and each one worth
one thousand dollars free and clear when the notes
get paid. And Billy Johnson's into logging
off the property, and he'll make more than anyone!
Mister Polk, take my advice, go home, give up
bein' the Presydent. Go home and buy
before it's done!"

     He looks at me and says, "I have!
Didn't you know? I've done it all, already!"

So the goak's on me. And does he have a laugh!

November 1848

A Military Campaign

As we approach the millennium, the judgments of God
are changing. From purely spiritual ones that purify
the church—the holy, saving remnant—they shift
to public ones that will purge the length and breadth
of this society.

           The root of evil in human
nature is here for all to see. But much
of what we see as sin is ignorance—not knowing
God, His ways, His saving grace. But think
of the telegraph! More and more people can be saved, the
        miserable
tally of salvation in our time may be transformed!

I have made a calculation: with our growing efforts, at the
        millennium
there will be but one lost soul for every seventeen
thousand four hundred sixty-five and one-third
souls whom we have saved!

           Christians, we must make
the supreme effort! We must put down vice and error of every
kind, we must promote the cause of truth
and everlasting righteousness—but this will only happen
if we wage a full-out military campaign!

           Let us now
embark on a great crusade. Hail, matchless heroes!
Our general has sacrificed his life already in this noble

cause. Apostles, prophets, martyrs of the past
have marched before us. They have conquered death and reign
with Jesus.

        The world now calls the victory of General
Scott in Mexico a glorious one. But surely
ours will be supreme, written on the vault
of God's great heaven in letters blazing like the prophets'.
An everlasting beacon! A never-fading splendor!

The Reverend Jonathan Edwards III
December 1848

Letter to the President

Dear Sir,

We have learned from the newspapers that the secretary of war has brought you specimens of the gold ore which was discovered last July near Sutter's Fort. We understand that you will now send these specimens to the Philadelphia mint so that they may be rendered and coined. We commend you for this act. It is an admirable gesture, demonstrating both public-spiritedness and thrift.

Given the reported size of the gold fields and the wealth which must surely pour out of them, we now ask, what shall be their true benefit to this nation?

Word of the presence of gold and silver is already generating wild enthusiasm among the populace. In this we see, on the one hand, the greatest opportunity this nation has yet known for the application of the spirit of enterprise. Churches, banks, stores, schools, and members of the learned professions must surely follow in the train of the thousands of prospectors and miners who are already en route to the California territory.

On the other hand, we see that the discovery of rich lodes of gold and silver shall bring with them temptations—faro dealers, cardsharks of all kinds, loose women, vendors of all manner of spirits—negus, toddies, pulls, and swills, to mention but a few—and after these will surely come the purveyors of circuses, menageries, minstrel shows, singers, dancers, ventriloquists, magicians, Madagascar manmonkeys, learned dogs, mammoth bears, jugglers, acrobats, Indiarubber men, trumpet blowers, bell ringers, sword swallowers, giants, dwarfs, Laplanders, adepts of Professor Faber's euphonium and speaking automaton, African bushmen, panoramas, fandango dancing, Chinese opera, theatrical companies, etcetera, etcetera.

Will our newly acquired Western Commonwealth be one in which the odor of righteousness and temperance may be perceived to waft from the daily life of its citizens?

Or will that commonwealth become a vile confusion of disarticulated interests held together by the blind forces of chance, greed, and immorality?

Surely you, in your last weeks as our president, can act to influence the outcome of this matter. Will California be permitted by executive inaction to become an exercise in careless living, drunkenness, the frivolity of endless entertainments, and decisions which are made by the turn of a card?

Prayerfully we have come to believe that your action in this matter is of vital importance.

You will influence what will be the nature of that destiny, that manifest destiny, which has been—and is being—revealed to us.

With our deepest respect and admiration,
We are yours truly,

>The Board of Governors,
>The American Tract Society

Philadelphia, Pennsylvania

[*Noted at the bottom, in Polk's hand:*]

James—Retain this. Pass it on to Taylor's people in March. Let Taylor undertake the reply. Is he not famous for his abilities as a commander?

[*In another, unknown hand from a much later date:*]

Practical politics consists in ignoring facts.

December 1848

Afterword

Of the characters depicted here a reader well might ask, "Whatever happened to them later on?"

As a result of the Whig victory in the elections of 1848, those who served as *advisers* to president Polk were obliged to find employment as the legislative representatives of steamship companies and railroads until the Democratic Party was returned to office after the election of Franklin Pierce in 1853. *Senator Daniel Webster's* life and career were hardly over in 1848. He persisted, and in 1852 he died of cirrhosis of the liver, murmuring, "I still live." *Moses Beach* was obsessed with speed and experimented with carrier pigeons, steam-powered presses, packet boats, and special trains in order to make the *Sun*'s reporting of news more timely. He succeeded. He died in 1868. *Anne Royall* was America's first female newspaper editor and publisher. She was known slightingly as the "Miss Flite" of the Capitol and wrote some two thousand pen portraits before she died in poverty in 1854. Her views appear much more valuable to us today than they did to many persons of her time. *General Sam Houston* wanted all of Mexico as a U.S. protectorate. Overall, however, he was a moderate in his political views and opposed secession. He died three weeks after the fall of Vicksburg, in 1863, and was called "a hoary-haired traitor" by many in the South. *Elias Howe* found little interest in his invention, the sewing machine, in the United States. It caught on in England when it was first adapted as a machine for sewing leather. He died in 1867. *John Charles Frémont* eventually returned to California, made a fortune in gold mining, became a senator from the state and then the first candidate of the Republican Party for the presidency, in 1856. He took bankruptcy in 1870 and his whole career then became a tragic anticlimax. He died in a rooming house in 1890. *General Zachary Taylor* succeeded James K. Polk as our twelfth president in 1849. He, too, owned a cotton plantation. He died in office in 1850, apparently from eating tainted fruit, and was succeeded by his eminently forgettable vice president, Millard Fillmore. *James K. Polk* felt that duty required him to supervise the whole of the operations of his government. He died in June of 1849, three months after leaving office, apparently of exhaustion. *Abraham Alfonse Albert Gallatin* turned his attention to the study of ethnology before he died in 1849. *Ralph Waldo Emerson* went to England in the summer of 1847. There he became famous as an American philosopher and lecturer, a fact that, in the curious workings of Anglo-American culture, served to confirm a similar fame in the United States. He died in 1882. Quaker *Levi Coffin* continued to work for the cause of freeing slaves, and after the Civil War worked on behalf of freedmen. He died in 1877. *Frederick Douglass* came back to the United States in 1847 to buy his own freedom. He had a long career as an abolitionist, journalist, and speaker, and was an early supporter of woman suffrage. After the Civil War he served as the U.S. minister to Haiti. He died in 1895. *John Quincy Adams*'s abilities in debate made his oratorical attacks something to be feared, even when he was an old man. *James Beckwourth* continued his adventures on the frontier. He wrote an occasional truth in his *Autobiography,* published in 1856. He participated in the Sand Creek Massacre in 1864 and died near Denver in 1867. *Margaret Fuller* sailed back to the United States with her husband and baby and on July 19, 1850, the three were drowned in a shipwreck off Fire Island, New York. Her friend Henry David Thoreau (whom she addressed as "Dear Ugly") made the journey to search for her body and the manuscript of her history of the Roman revolution. In the end, only the baby's body was recovered. The person who called himself *Ray Ennersly* seems to have gone on to become the bishop of a church that he himself founded. There is a rumor that in later years he became the lieutenant governor of Santo Domingo. If true, he would have met *Jane McManus Storms* there. She emigrated to Santo Domingo, operated a pineapple plantation, and worked ceaselessly if unsuccessfully to make Santo Domingo a state of the Union. *"Major Seb Simon"* was purported to be the pen name of a female recluse in Maine. After serving in the Confederate army during the Civil War, *Doctor Josiah C. Nott* wrote a confident and authoritative monograph on bone and joint injuries sustained in battle. He also became famous as the founder of the science of "niggerology." He died in 1873. *Isaac H. Dismukes* and *John A. Mairs* used the money they skimmed from the operation of President Polk's plantation in Mississippi to buy forty acres each in Alabama. Prof. *Louis Agassiz* brought luster and international repute to the faculty of natural sciences at Harvard College for many decades. He once described Harvard as "a respectable high school where they teach the dregs of education." He died in 1893. *Harriet Beecher Stowe* published *Uncle Tom's Cabin* in serial form in 1851–52. President Lincoln is said to have exclaimed on meeting her for the first time, "So you are the little lady who started this war." She lived until 1896. The records are unclear, but it appears that a person named *Lud Jessup* established himself as a faro dealer in the western goldfields, then appears to have been elected sheriff of notorious Mariposa County, California, and then disappeared. *General Winfield Scott* resigned his commission before the court of inquiry finished its work. Robert E. Lee, one of Scott's brilliant lieutenants, said that Scott "was turned out as an old horse to die." Scott was eventually restored to rank in 1855, after running as the Whig candidate for president in 1852 and having been defeated by Franklin Pierce, another easily forgettable American president. Scott died in 1866. *Andrew Jackson Davis* had his first mesmeric flight through space in 1844. Thereafter he gave 157 lectures on the topic in New York City between 1845 and 1847. The "Seer of Poughkeepsie" rode the crest of the wave of fascination with spiritualism in America until his death in 1910, by which time he was the author of twenty-six books on the subject. Senator *Thomas Hart*

Benton, who was continually looking out for the restoration of the reputation of his son-in-law, John Charles Frémont, suffered a "dethronement" in the Senate and lost his seat to a Whig in 1850. He died in 1858. *Theodore Parker* found that the antislavery cause was strenuous, exciting, and profitable. He died in Florence, Italy, in 1860. There are no records that *Samuel Chilton* actually embarked on or returned from the trip to explore Indian mounds near the Ohio River, to which he referred in his letter. Prof. *Charles White, M.D.,* left the United States for Canada shortly after the conclusion of the colloquy, and there is no further record of him. Mr. *Phineas Cheveux* continued his trichological investigations until he was fatally injured one day in 1851 while taking a hair sample from the tail of a Texas mustang. *Orson Fowler,* abetted by his brother, Lorenzo, charmed ignorant audiences by his assumption of scientific knowledge and by the extreme sentimentality of his outlook on life. He died a wealthy man, in 1867. The *senator from Illinois* here referred to might have been Steven Douglas, but faulty stenographic transcription might have confused his name and state with that of Senator *Donovan O'Sullivan* of New York. *John Black* served long and ably in the consular service, but records do not indicate where. It is possible that served in Haiti during the period that Frederick Douglass was our ambassador there. Colonel *Bryant Blessing* kept a notebook during the time of his service in the Mexican War as well as the Civil War. All but the one page that is included here has been lost. *Horatio Greenough* was the first American sculptor to become an expatriate. He went to Italy to live and work. His statue of George Washington arrived in Washington in 1843 and was the butt of wiseacres and witlings until years later when it was finally housed in the building of the Smithsonian Institution. Greenough died in 1852. *Eliza Allen*'s innate modesty required her to assume this pseudonym at the time. Unfortunately, her true identity is unknown. *Brigham Young*'s success as a church leader and businessman enabled him to give polygamy a grace it had nowhere else and to make of the Mormon experiment an economic success despite the furious opposition of many. He died in 1877. *G. R. Glidden* eventually left Egyptology and became involved in a scheme to build a transoceanic railroad through Honduras. He he died in Honduras of yellow fever. The Right Reverend *P. T. Bainum,* D.D., was tragically killed the day after giving this prayer to the Senate by a runaway horse on Washington's Constitution Avenue. It was after the death of *Joseph Harrison* that Harrison's widow disposed of the Catlin Indian collection by giving it to the Smithsonian Institution, finally, in 1879. The Reverend *Moncure Conway* was an extremely young Methodist minister in 1848. When he had gained more maturity he became a Unitarian, edited *The Dial,* and was the author of some seventy books. *Michael Shiner* lived as a freedman should, keeping a diary of the events of his life and the lives of those around him. The Reverend *Jonathan Edwards III* continued to work in the vineyards in which his distinguished antecedents had toiled, but he was to live to see the advent of a new kind of preacher in the person of Henry Ward Beecher, whose oratorical style and organizational abilities quickly changed the face of urban Protestantism in the United States. As for the newspaper correspondents *S. L. C., M. B, Jr.,* and *C. D.,* their contributions remain mostly anonymous, as well as their lives. However, as they wrote at a time when the American newspaper was coming to be an important means of mass persuasion, they and their editors no doubt would have agreed with the sentiment ascribed to Anatole France and employed by the author in the writing of this book:

"All the historical books which contain no lies are extremely tedious."

DATE DUE
